THE BOX

UNCANNY STORIES

ALSO BY RICHARD MATHESON

The Beardless Warriors

Duel

Earthbound

Hell House

Hunted Past Reason

I Am Legend

The Incredible Shrinking Man

Nightmare at 20,000 Feet

Noir

Now You See It . . .

The Path: A New Look at Reality

7 Steps to Midnight

A Stir of Echoes

Somewhere in Time

What Dreams May Come

Journal of the Gun Years

The Memoirs of Wild Bill Hickok

THE BOX

UNCANNY STORIES

Richard Matheson

TOR®

A TOM DOHERTY ASSOCIATES BOOK

NEW YORK

THE BOX: UNCANNY STORIES

Copyright © 2008 by RXR, Inc.

All rights reserved.

Previously published by Tor Books under the title
Button, Button: Uncanny Stories

Book design by Spring Hoteling

A Tor Book
Published by Tom Doherty Associates, LLC
175 Fifth Avenue
New York, NY 10010

www.tor-forge.com

Tor® is a registered trademark of Tom Doherty Associates, LLC.

The Library of Congress has catalogued this trade paperback as follows:

Matheson, Richard, 1926–
    Button, button : uncanny stories / Richard Matheson.
        p. cm.
    "A Tom Doherty Associates book."
    ISBN-13: 978-0-7653-1257-0
    ISBN-10: 0-7653-1257-3
    I. Title.

PS3563.A8355 B86 2008
813'.54—dc22

                                                            2007047844

ISBN 978-0-7653-2171-8

First Edition: April 2008
Second Edition: September 2009

Printed in the United States of America

0 9 8 7 6 5 4 3 2 1

COPYRIGHT ACKNOWLEDGMENTS

With love to my son Richard, for protecting my life in every way.

CONTENTS

INTRODUCTION

A question often asked of writers is "Where did you get the idea for that story?" It is a question we can usually answer easily. I can answer it with regard to "Button, Button" because the idea came from my wife although, at the time, she had no idea she was doing it. Neither did I. That came later.

I will not tell you the idea prior to your reading of the story except to say that the idea was mentioned in a college psychology class my wife took. One idea in that class that I *can* mention is the following: To contribute importantly to world peace, would you walk down New York's Broadway—naked?

The idea, which resulted in my writing of "Button, Button" was of a similar nature: a sacrifice of human dignity in exchange for a specific goal—in this case nothing anywhere near as worthy as world peace.

RICHARD MATHESON
May 17, 2007

BUTTON, BUTTON

UNCANNY STORIES

BUTTON, BUTTON

The package was lying by the front door—a cube-shaped carton sealed with tape, the name and address printed by hand: MR. AND MRS. ARTHUR LEWIS, 217 E. 37TH STREET, NEW YORK, NEW YORK 10016. Norma picked it up, unlocked the door, and went into the apartment. It was just getting dark.

After she put the lamb chops in the broiler, she made herself a drink and sat down to open the package.

Inside the carton was a push-button unit fastened to a small wooden box. A glass dome covered the button. Norma tried to lift it off, but it was locked in place. She turned the unit over and saw a folded piece of paper Scotch-taped to the bottom of the box. She pulled it off: "Mr. Steward will call on you at eight p.m."

Norma put the button unit beside her on the couch. She sipped the drink and reread the typed note, smiling.

A few moments later, she went back into the kitchen to make the salad.

The doorbell rang at eight o'clock. "I'll get it," Norma called from the kitchen. Arthur was in the living room, reading.

There was a small man in the hallway. He removed his hat as Norma opened the door. "Mrs. Lewis?" he inquired politely.

"Yes?"

"I'm Mr. Steward."

"Oh, yes." Norma repressed a smile. She was sure now it was a sales pitch.

"May I come in?" asked Mr. Steward.

"I'm rather busy," Norma said. "I'll get you your watchamacallit, though." She started to turn.

"Don't you want to know what it is?"

Norma turned back. Mr. Steward's tone had been offensive. "No, I don't think so," she said.

"It could prove very valuable," he told her.

"Monetarily?" she challenged.

Mr. Steward nodded. "Monetarily," he said.

Norma frowned. She didn't like his attitude. "What are you trying to sell?" she asked.

"I'm not selling anything," he answered.

Arthur came out of the living room. "Something wrong?"

Mr. Steward introduced himself.

"Oh, the . . ." Arthur pointed toward the living room and smiled. "What is that gadget, anyway?"

"It won't take long to explain," replied Mr. Steward. "May I come in?"

"If you're selling something . . ." Arthur said.

Mr. Steward shook his head. "I'm not."

Arthur looked at Norma. "Up to you," she said.

He hesitated. "Well, why not?" he said.

They went into the living room and Mr. Steward sat in Norma's chair. He reached into an inside coat pocket and withdrew a small sealed envelope. "Inside here is a key to the bell-unit dome," he said. He set the envelope on the chairside table. "The bell is connected to our office."

"What's it for?" asked Arthur.

"If you push the button," Mr. Steward told him, "somewhere in the world, someone you don't know will die. In return for which you will receive a payment of fifty thousand dollars."

Norma stared at the small man. He was smiling.

"What are you talking about?" Arthur asked him.

Mr. Steward looked surprised. "But I've just explained," he said.

"Is this a practical joke?" asked Arthur.

"Not at all. The offer is completely genuine."

"You aren't making sense," Arthur said. "You expect us to believe . . ."

"Whom do you represent?" demanded Norma.

Mr. Steward looked embarrassed. "I'm afraid I'm not at liberty to tell you that," he said. "However, I assure you the organization is of international scope."

"I think you'd better leave," Arthur said, standing.

Mr. Steward rose. "Of course."

"And take your button unit with you."

"Are you sure you wouldn't care to think about it for a day or so?"

Arthur picked up the button unit and the envelope and thrust them into Mr. Steward's hands. He walked into the hall and pulled open the door.

"I'll leave my card," said Mr. Steward. He placed it on the table by the door.

When he was gone, Arthur tore it in half and tossed the pieces onto the table. "God!" he said.

Norma was still sitting on the sofa. "What do you think it was?" she asked.

"I don't care to know," he answered.

She tried to smile but couldn't. "Aren't you curious at all?"

"No." He shook his head.

After Arthur returned to his book, Norma went back to the kitchen and finished washing the dishes.

Why won't you talk about it?" Norma asked later.

Arthur's eyes shifted as he brushed his teeth. He looked at her reflection in the bathroom mirror.

"Doesn't it intrigue you?"

"It offends me," Arthur said.

"I know, but—" Norma rolled another curler in her hair "—doesn't it intrigue you, too?"

"You think it's a practical joke?" she asked as they went into the bedroom.

"If it is, it's a sick one."

Norma sat on the bed and took off her slippers.

"Maybe it's some kind of psychological research."

Arthur shrugged. "Could be."

"Maybe some eccentric millionaire is doing it."

"Maybe."

"Wouldn't you like to know?"

Arthur shook his head.

"Why?"

"Because it's immoral," he told her.

Norma slid beneath the covers. "Well, I think it's intriguing," she said.

Arthur turned off the lamp and leaned over to kiss her. "Good night," he said.

"Good night." She patted his back.

Norma closed her eyes. Fifty thousand dollars, she thought.

In the morning, as she left the apartment, Norma saw the card halves on the table. Impulsively, she dropped them into her purse. She locked the front door and joined Arthur in the elevator.

While she was on her coffee break, she took the card halves from her purse and held the torn edges together. Only Mr. Steward's name and telephone number were printed on the card.

After lunch, she took the card halves from her purse again and Scotch-taped the edges together. Why am I doing this? she thought.

Just before five, she dialed the number.

"Good afternoon," said Mr. Steward's voice.

Norma almost hung up but restrained herself. She cleared her throat. "This is Mrs. Lewis," she said.

"Yes, Mrs. Lewis." Mr. Steward sounded pleased.

"I'm curious."

"That's natural," Mr. Steward said.

"Not that I believe a word of what you told us."

"Oh, it's quite authentic," Mr. Steward answered.

"Well, whatever . . ." Norma swallowed. "When you said someone in the world would die, what did you mean?"

"Exactly that," he answered. "It could be anyone. All we guarantee is that you don't know them. And, of course, that you wouldn't have to watch them die."

"For fifty thousand dollars," Norma said.

"That is correct."

She made a scoffing sound. "That's crazy."

"Nonetheless, that is the proposition," Mr. Steward said. "Would you like me to return the button unit?"

Norma stiffened. "Certainly not." She hung up angrily.

The package was lying by the front door; Norma saw it as she left the elevator. Well, of all the nerve, she thought. She glared at the carton as she unlocked the door. I just won't take it in, she thought. She went inside and started dinner.

Later, she carried her drink to the front hall. Opening the door, she picked up the package and carried it into the kitchen, leaving it on the table.

She sat in the living room, sipping her drink and looking out the window. After awhile, she went back into the kitchen to turn the cutlets in the broiler. She put the package in a bottom cabinet. She'd throw it out in the morning.

Maybe some eccentric millionaire is playing games with people," she said.

Arthur looked up from his dinner. "I don't understand you."

"What does that mean?"

"Let it go," he told her.

Norma ate in silence. Suddenly, she put her fork down. "Suppose it's a genuine offer," she said.

Arthur stared at her.

"Suppose it's a genuine offer."

"All right, suppose it is!" He looked incredulous. "What would you like to do? Get the button back and push it? Murder someone?"

Norma looked disgusted. "Murder."

"How would *you* define it?"

"If you don't even know the person?" Norma asked.

Arthur looked astounded. "Are you saying what I think you are?"

"If it's some old Chinese peasant ten thousand miles away? Some diseased native in the Congo?"

"How about some baby boy in Pennsylvania?" Arthur countered. "Some beautiful little girl on the next block?"

"Now you're loading things."

"The point is, Norma," he continued, "that *who* you kill makes no difference. It's still murder."

"The point is," Norma broke in, "if it's someone you've never seen in your life and never will see, someone whose death you don't even have to know about, you still wouldn't push the button?"

Arthur stared at her, appalled. "You mean you would?"

"Fifty thousand dollars, Arthur."

"What has the amount—"

"Fifty thousand dollars, Arthur," Norma interrupted. "A chance to take that trip to Europe we've always talked about."

"Norma, no."

"A chance to buy that cottage on the Island."

"Norma, no." His face was white. "For God's sake, no!"

She shuddered. "All right, take it easy," she said. "Why are you getting so upset? It's only talk."

After dinner, Arthur went into the living room. Before he left the table, he said, "I'd rather not discuss it anymore, if you don't mind."

Norma shrugged. "Fine with me."

She got up earlier than usual to make pancakes, eggs, and bacon for Arthur's breakfast.

"What's the occasion?" he asked with a smile.

"No occasion." Norma looked offended. "I wanted to do it, that's all."

"Good," he said. "I'm glad you did."

She refilled his cup. "Wanted to show you I'm not . . ." She shrugged.

"Not what?"

"Selfish."

"Did I say you were?"

"Well—" She gestured vaguely. "—last night . . ."

Arthur didn't speak.

"All that talk about the button," Norma said. "I think you—well, misunderstood me."

"In what way?" His voice was guarded.

"I think you felt—" She gestured again. "—that I was only thinking of myself."

"Oh."

"I wasn't."

"Norma."

"Well, I wasn't. When I talked about Europe, a cottage on the Island . . ."

"Norma, why are we getting so involved in this?"

"I'm not involved at all." She drew in a shaking breath. "I'm simply trying to indicate that . . ."

"What?"

"That I'd like for us to go to Europe. Like for us to have a nicer apartment, nicer furniture, nicer clothes. Like for us to finally have a baby, for that matter."

"Norma, we will," he said.

"When?"

He stared at her in dismay. "Norma . . ."

"When?"

"Are you—" He seemed to draw back slightly. "Are you really saying . . . ?"

"I'm saying that they're probably doing it for some research project!" she cut him off. "That they want to know what average people would do under such a circumstance! That they're just saying someone would die, in order to study reactions, see if there'd be guilt, anxiety, whatever! You don't really think they'd kill somebody, do you?"

Arthur didn't answer. She saw his hands trembling. After awhile, he got up and left.

When he'd gone to work, Norma remained at the table, staring into her coffee. I'm going to be late, she thought. She shrugged. What difference did it make? She should be home anyway, not working in an office.

While she was stacking the dishes, she turned abruptly, dried her hands, and took the package from the bottom cabinet. Opening it, she set the button unit on the table. She stared at it for a long time before taking the key from its envelope and removing the glass dome. She stared at the button. How ridiculous, she thought. All this over a meaningless button.

Reaching out, she pressed it down. For us, she thought angrily.

She shuddered. Was it happening? A chill of horror swept across her.

In a moment, it had passed. She made a contemptuous noise. Ridiculous, she thought. To get so worked up over nothing.

She had just turned the supper steaks and was making herself another drink when the telephone rang. She picked it up. "Hello?"

"Mrs. Lewis?"

"Yes?"

"This is the Lenox Hill Hospital."

She felt unreal as the voice informed her of the subway accident, the shoving crowd. Arthur pushed from the platform in front of the train. She was conscious of shaking her head but couldn't stop.

As she hung up, she remembered Arthur's life insurance policy for $25,000, with double indemnity for—

"No." She couldn't seem to breathe. She struggled to her feet and walked into the kitchen numbly. Something cold pressed at her skull as she removed the button unit from the wastebasket. There were no nails or screws visible. She couldn't see how it was put together.

Abruptly, she began to smash it on the sink edge, pounding it harder and harder, until the wood split. She pulled the sides apart, cutting her fingers without noticing. There were no transistors in the box, no wires or tubes. The box was empty.

She whirled with a gasp as the telephone rang. Stumbling into the living room, she picked up the receiver.

"Mrs. Lewis?" Mr. Steward asked.

It wasn't her voice shrieking so; it couldn't be. "You said I wouldn't know the one that died!"

"My dear lady," Mr. Steward said, "do you really think you knew your husband?"

GIRL OF MY DREAMS

He woke up, grinning, in the darkness. Carrie was having a nightmare. He lay on his side and listened to her breathless moaning. Must be a good one, he thought. He reached out and touched her back. The nightgown was wet with her perspiration. Great, he thought. He pulled his hand away as she squirmed against it, starting to make faint noises in her throat; it sounded as if she were trying to say "No."

No, hell, Greg thought. Dream, you ugly bitch; what else are you good for? He yawned and pulled his left arm from beneath the covers. Three-sixteen. He wound the watch stem sluggishly. Going to get me one of those electric watches one of these days, he thought. Maybe this dream would do it. Too bad Carrie had no control over them. If she did, he could really make it big.

He rolled onto his back. The nightmare was ending now; or coming to its peak, he was never sure which. What difference did it make anyway? He wasn't interested in the machinery, just the product. He grinned again, reaching over to the bedside table for his cigarettes. Lighting one, he blew out smoke. Now he'd have to comfort her, he thought with a frown. That was the part he could live without.

Dumb little creep. Why couldn't she be blonde and beautiful? He expelled a burst of smoke. Well, you couldn't ask for everything. If she were good-looking, she probably wouldn't have these dreams. There were plenty of other women to provide the rest of it.

Carrie jerked violently and sat up with a cry, pulling the covers from his legs. Greg looked at her outline in the darkness. She was shivering. "Oh, no," she whispered. He watched her head begin to shake. "No. No." She started to cry, her body hitching with sobs. Oh, Christ, he thought, this'll take hours. Irritably, he pressed his cigarette into the ashtray and sat up.

"Baby?" he said.

She twisted around with a gasp and stared at him. "Come 'ere," he told her. He opened his arms and she flung herself against him. He could feel her narrow fingers gouging at his back, the soggy weight of her breasts against his chest. Oh, boy, he thought. He kissed her neck, grimacing at the smell of her sweat-damp skin. Oh, boy, what I go through. He caressed her back. "Take it easy, baby," he said, "I'm here." He let her cling to him, sobbing weakly. "Bad dream?" he asked. He tried to sound concerned.

"Oh, Greg." She could barely speak. "It was horrible, oh, God, how horrible."

He grinned. It *was* a good one.

W hich way?" he asked.

Carrie perched stiffly on the edge of the seat, looking through the windshield with troubled eyes. Any second now, she'd pretend she didn't know; she always did. Greg's fingers tightened slowly on the wheel. One of these days, by God, he'd smack her right across her ugly face and walk out, free. Damn freak. He felt the skin begin to tighten across his cheeks. "Well?" he asked.

"I don't—"

"*Which way, Carrie?*" God, he'd like to twist back one of her scrawny arms and break the damn thing; squeeze that skinny neck until her breath stopped.

Carrie swallowed dryly. "Left," she murmured.

Bingo! Greg almost laughed aloud, slapping down the turn indicator. *Left*—right into the Eastridge area, the money area. You dreamed it right this time, you dog, he thought; this is *It*. All he had to do now was play it smart and he'd be free of her for good. He'd sweated it out and now it was payday!

The tires made a crisp sound on the pavement as he turned the car onto the quiet, tree-lined street. "How far?" he asked. She didn't answer and he looked at her threateningly. Her eyes were shut.

"How far? I said."

Carrie clutched her hands together. "Greg, please—" she started. Tears were squeezing out beneath her lids.

"Damn it!"

Carrie whimpered and said something. "What?" he snapped. She drew in a wavering breath. "The middle of the next block," she said.

"Which side?"

"The right."

Greg smiled. He leaned back against the seat and re-laxed. That was more like it. Dumb bitch tried the same old

"I-forget" routine every time. When would she learn that he had her down cold? He almost chuckled. She never would, he thought; because, after this one, he'd be gone and she could dream for nothing.

"Tell me when we reach it," he said.

"Yes," she answered. She had turned her face to the window and was leaning her forehead against the cold glass. Don't cool it too much, he thought, amused; keep it hot for Daddy. He pressed away the rising smile as she turned to look at him. Was she picking up on him? Or was it just the usual? It was always the same. Just before they reached wherever they were going, she'd look at him intently as if to convince herself that it was worth the pain. He felt like laughing in her face. Obviously, it was worth it. How else could a beast like her land someone with his class? Except for him, her bed would be the emptiest, her nights the longest.

"Almost there?" he asked.

Carrie looked to the front again. "The white one," she said.

"With the half-circle drive?"

She nodded tightly. "Yes."

Greg clenched his teeth, a spasm of avidity sweeping through him. Fifty thousand if it was worth a nickel, he thought. Oh, you bitch, you crazy bitch, you really nailed it for me this time! He turned the wheel and pulled in at the curb. Cutting the engine, he glanced across the street. The convertible would come from that direction, he thought. He wondered who'd be driving it. Not that it mattered.

"Greg?"

He turned and eyed her coldly. "What?"

She bit her lip, then started to speak.

"*No*," he said, cutting her off. He pulled out the ignition key and shoved open the door. "Let's go," he said. He slid out, shut the door and walked around the car. Carrie was still inside. "Let's *go,* baby," he said, the hint of venom in his voice.

"Greg, please—"

He shuddered at the cost of repressing an intense desire to scream curses at her, jerk open the door and drag her out by her hair. His rigid fingers clamped on the handle and he opened the door, waited. Christ, but she was ugly—the features, the skin, the body. She'd never looked so repugnant to him. "*I said let's go,*" he told her. He couldn't disguise the tremble of fury in his voice.

Carrie got out and he shut the door. It was getting colder. Greg drew up the collar of his topcoat, shivering as they started up the drive toward the front door of the house. He could use a heavier coat, he thought; with a nice, thick lining. A real sharp one, maybe black. He'd get one one of these days—and maybe real soon, too. He glanced at Carrie, wondering if she had any notion of his plans. He doubted it even though she looked more worried than ever. What the hell was with her? She'd never been this bad before. Was it because it was a kid? He shrugged. What difference did it make? She'd perform.

"Cheer up," he said. "It's a school day. You won't have to see him." She didn't answer.

They went up two steps onto the brick porch and stopped before the door. Greg pushed the button and, deep inside the house, melodic chimes sounded. While they waited, he reached inside his topcoat pocket and touched the small leather notebook. Funny how he always felt like some kind of weird salesman when they were operating. A salesman with a damned closed market, he thought, amused. No one else could offer what he had to sell, that was for sure.

He glanced at Carrie. "Cheer *up*," he told her. "We're helping them, aren't we?"

Carrie shivered. "It won't be too much, will it, Greg?"

"I'll decide on—"

He broke off as the door was opened. For a moment, he felt angry disappointment that the bell had not been answered by a maid. Then he thought: Oh, what the hell, the money's still here—and he smiled at the woman who stood before them. "Good afternoon," he said.

The woman looked at him with that half polite, half suspicious smile most women gave him at first. "Yes?" she asked.

"It's about Paul," he said.

The smile disappeared, the woman's face grew blank. "What?" she asked.

"That's your son's name, isn't it?"

The woman glanced at Carrie. Already, she was disconcerted, Greg could see.

"He's in danger of his life," he told her. "Are you interested in hearing more about it?"

"What's happened to him?"

Greg smiled affably. "Nothing yet," he answered. The woman caught her breath as if, abruptly, she were being strangled.

"You've taken him," she murmured.

Greg's smile broadened. "Nothing like that," he said.

"Where is he then?" the woman asked.

Greg looked at his wristwatch, feigning surprise. "Isn't he at school?" he asked.

Uneasily confused, the woman stared at him for several moments before she twisted away, pushing at the door. Greg caught hold of it before it shut. "Inside," he ordered.

"Can't we wait out—?"

Carrie broke off with a gasp as he clamped his fingers on her arm and pulled her into the hall. While he shut the door, Greg listened to the rapid whir and click of a telephone being dialed in the kitchen. He smiled and took hold of Carrie's arm again, guiding her into the living room. "Sit," he told her.

Carrie settled gingerly on the edge of a chair while he appraised the room. Money was in evidence wherever he looked, in the carpeting and drapes, the period furniture, the accessories. Greg pulled in a tight, exultant breath and tried to keep from grinning like an eager kid; this was *It* all right. Dropping onto the sofa, he stretched luxuriously, leaned back and crossed his legs, glancing at the name on a magazine lying on the end table beside him. In the kitchen, he could hear the woman saying, "He's in Room Fourteen; Mrs. Jennings' class."

A sudden clicking sound made Carrie gasp. Greg turned his head and saw, through the back drapes, a collie scratching at the sliding-glass door; beyond, he noted, with renewed pleasure, the glint of swimming pool water. Greg watched the dog. It must be the one that would—

"*Thank* you," said the woman gratefully. Greg turned back and looked in that direction. The woman hung up the telephone receiver and her footsteps tapped across the kitchen floor, becoming soundless as she stepped onto the hallway carpeting. She started cautiously toward the front door.

"We're in here, Mrs. Wheeler," said Greg.

The woman caught her breath and whirled in shock. "What *is* this?" she demanded.

"Is he all right?" Greg asked.

"What do you want?"

Greg drew the notebook from his pocket and held it out. "Would you like to look at this?" he asked.

The woman didn't answer but peered at Greg through narrowing eyes. "That's right," he said. "We're selling something."

The woman's face grew hard.

"*Your son's life,*" Greg completed.

The woman gaped at him, momentary resentment invaded by fear again. Jesus, you look stupid, Greg felt like telling her. He forced a smile. "Are you interested?" he asked.

"Get out of here before I call the police." The woman's voice was husky, tremulous.

"You're not interested in your son's life then?"

The woman shivered with fear-ridden anger. "Did you hear me?" she said.

Greg exhaled through clenching teeth.

"Mrs. Wheeler," he said, "unless you listen to us—*carefully*—your son will soon be dead." From the corners of his eyes, he noticed Carrie wincing and felt like smashing in her face. That's right, he thought with savage fury. Show her how scared you are, you stupid bitch!

Mrs. Wheeler's lips stirred falteringly as she stared at Greg. "What are you talking about?" she finally asked.

"Your son's life, Mrs. Wheeler."

"Why should you want to hurt my boy?" the woman asked, a sudden quaver in her voice. Greg felt himself relax. She was almost in the bag.

"Did I say that we were going to hurt him?" he asked, smiling at her quizzically. "I don't remember saying that, Mrs. Wheeler."

"Then—?"

"Sometime before the middle of the month," Greg interrupted, "Paul will be run over by a car and killed."

"What?"

Greg did not repeat.

"What car?" asked the woman. She looked at Greg in panic. "What car?" she demanded.

"We don't know exactly."

"Where?" the woman asked. "When?"

"That information," Greg replied, "is what we're selling."

The woman turned to Carrie, looking at her frightenedly. Carrie lowered her gaze, teeth digging at her lower lip. The woman looked back at Greg as he continued.

"Let me explain," he said. "My wife is what's known as a 'sensitive.' You may not be familiar with the term. It means she has visions and dreams. Very often, they have to do with real people. Like the dream she had last night—about your son."

The woman shrank from his words and, as Greg expected,

an element of shrewdness modified her expression; there was now, in addition to fear, suspicion.

"I know what you're thinking," he informed her. "Don't waste your time. Look at this notebook and you'll see—"

"Get out of here," the woman said.

Greg's smile grew strained. "That again?" he asked. "You mean you really don't care about your son's life?"

The woman managed a smile of contempt. "Shall I call the police now?" she asked. "The *bunco* squad?"

"If you really want to," answered Greg, "but I suggest you listen to me first." He opened the notebook and began to read. "*January twenty-second: Man named Jim to fall from roof while adjusting television aerial. Ramsay Street. Two-story house, green with white trim.* Here's the news item."

Greg glanced at Carrie and nodded once, ignoring her pleading look as he stood and walked across the room. The woman cringed back apprehensively but didn't move. Greg held up the notebook page. "As you can see," he said, "the man didn't believe what we told him and did fall off his roof on January twenty-second; it's harder to convince them when you can't give any details so as not to give it all away." He clucked as if disturbed. "He should have paid us, though," he said. "It would have been a lot less expensive than a broken back."

"Who do you think you're—?"

"Here's another," Greg said, turning a page. "This should interest you. *February twelfth, afternoon: Boy, 13, name unknown, to fall into abandoned well shaft, fracture pelvis. Lives on Darien Circle*, et cetera, et cetera, you can see the details here," he finished, pointing at the page. "Here's the newspaper clipping. As you can see, his parents were just in time. They'd refused to pay at first, threatened to call the police like you did." He smiled at the woman. "Threw us out of the house as a matter of fact," he said. "On the afternoon of the twelfth, though, when I made a last-minute phone check, they were out of their minds with worry. Their son had disappeared and they had no idea where he was—I hadn't mentioned the well shaft, of course."

He paused for a moment of dramatic emphasis, enjoying the moment fully. "I went over to their house," he said. "They made their payment and I told them where their son was." He pointed at the clipping. "He was found, as you see—down in an abandoned well shaft. With a broken pelvis."

"Do you really—?"

"—expect you to believe all this?" Greg completed her thought. "Not completely; no one ever does at first. Let me tell you what you're thinking right now. You're thinking that we cut out these newspaper items and made up this story to fit them. You're entitled to believe that if you want to—" his face hardened "—but, if you do, you'll have a dead son by the middle of the month, you can count on that."

He smiled cheerfully. "I don't believe you'd enjoy hearing how it's going to happen," he said.

The smile began to fade. "And it *is* going to happen, Mrs. Wheeler, whether you believe it or not."

The woman, still too dazed by fright to be completely sure of her suspicion, watched Greg as he turned to Carrie. "Well?" he said.

"I don't—"

"*Let's have it,*" he demanded.

Carrie bit her lower lip and tried to restrain the sob.

"What are you going to do?" the woman asked.

Greg turned to her with a smile. "Make our point," he said. He looked at Carrie again. "*Well?*"

She answered, eyes closed, voice pained and feeble. "There's a throw rug by the nursery door," she said. "You'll slip on it while you're carrying the baby."

Greg glanced at her in pleased surprise; he hadn't known there was a baby. Quickly, he looked at the woman as Carrie continued in a troubled voice, "There's a black widow spider underneath the playpen on the patio, it will bite the baby, there's a—"

"Care to check these items, Mrs. Wheeler?" Greg broke in. Suddenly, he hated her for her slowness, for her failure to accept. "Or shall we just walk out of here," he said, sharply, "*and let that blue convertible drag Paul's head along the street until his brains spill out?*"

The woman looked at him in horror. Greg felt a momentary dread that he had told her too much, then relaxed as he realized that he hadn't. "I suggest you check," he told her, pleasantly. The woman backed away from him a little bit, then turned and hurried toward the patio door. "Oh, incidentally," Greg said, remembering. She turned. "That dog out there will try to save your son but it won't succeed; the car will kill it, too."

The woman stared at him, as if uncomprehending, then turned away and, sliding open the patio door, went outside. Greg saw the collie frisking around her as she moved across the patio. Leisurely, he returned to the sofa and sat down.

"Greg—?"

He frowned grimacingly, jerking up his hand to silence her. Out on the patio, there was a scraping noise as the woman overturned the playpen. He listened intently. There was a sudden gasp, then the stamping of the woman's shoe on concrete, an excited barking by the dog. Greg smiled and leaned back with a sigh. Bingo.

When the woman came back in, he smiled at her, noticing how heavily she breathed.

"That could happen any place," she said, defensively.

"Could it?" Greg's smile remained intact. "And the throw rug?"

"Maybe you looked around while I was in the kitchen."

"We didn't."

"Maybe you guessed."

"And maybe we didn't," he told her, chilling his smile. "Maybe everything we've said is true. You want to gamble on it?"

The woman had no reply. Greg looked at Carrie. "Anything else?" he asked. Carrie shivered fitfully. "An electric outlet by the baby's crib," she said. "She has a bobby pin beside her, she's been trying to put it in the plug and—"

"Mrs. Wheeler?" Greg looked inquisitively at the woman. He snickered as she turned and hurried from the room. When she was gone, he smiled and winked at Carrie. "You're really on today, baby," he said. She returned his look with glistening eyes. "Greg, please don't make it too much," she murmured.

Greg turned away from her, the smile withdrawn. Relax, he told himself; relax. After today, you'll be free of her.

Casually, he slipped the notebook back into his topcoat pocket.

The woman returned in several minutes, her expression now devoid of anything but dread. Between two fingers of her right hand she was carrying a bobby pin. "*How did you know?*" she asked. Her voice was hollow with dismay.

"I believe I explained that, Mrs. Wheeler," Greg replied. "My wife has a gift. She knows exactly where and when the accident will occur. Do you care to buy that information?"

The woman's hands twitched at her sides. "What do you want?" she asked.

"Ten thousand dollars in cash," Greg answered. His fingers flexed reactively as Carrie gasped but he didn't look at her. He fixed his gaze on the woman's stricken face. "Ten thousand . . ." she repeated dumbly.

"That's correct. Is it a deal?"

"But we don't—"

"*Take it or leave it, Mrs. Wheeler.* You're not in a bargaining position. Don't think for a second that there's anything you can do to prevent the accident. Unless you know the exact time and place, it's going to happen." He stood abruptly, causing her to start. "Well?" he snapped, "what's it going to be? Ten thousand dollars or your son's life?"

The woman couldn't answer. Greg's eyes flicked to where Carrie sat in mute despair. "Let's go," he said. He started for the hall.

"*Wait.*"

Greg turned and looked at the woman. "Yes?"

"How—do I know—?" she faltered.

"You don't," he broke in; "you don't know a thing. *We do.*"

He waited another few moments for her decision, then walked into the kitchen and, removing his memo pad from an inside pocket, slipped the pencil free and jotted down the telephone number. He heard the woman murmuring pleadingly to Carrie and, shoving the pad and pencil into his top-coat pocket, left the kitchen. "Let's go," he said to Carrie who was standing now. He glanced disinterestedly at the woman. "I'll phone this afternoon," he said. "You can tell me then what you and your husband have decided to do." His mouth went hard. "*It'll be the only call you'll get,*" he said.

He turned and walked to the front door, opened it. "Come on, come on," he ordered irritably. Carrie slipped by him, brushing at the tears on her cheeks. Greg followed and began to close the door, then stopped as if remembering something.

"Incidentally," he said. He smiled at the woman. "I wouldn't call the police if I were you. There's nothing they could charge us with even if they found us. And, of course, we couldn't tell you then—and your son would have to die." He closed the door and started for the car, a picture of the woman printed in his mind: standing, dazed and trembling, in her living room, looking at him with haunted eyes. Greg grunted in amusement.

She was hooked.

Greg drained his glass and fell back heavily on the sofa arm, making a face. It was the last cheap whiskey he'd ever drink;

from now on, it was exclusively the best. He turned his head to look at Carrie. She was standing by the window of their hotel living room, staring at the city. What the hell was she brooding about now? Likely, she was wondering where that blue convertable was. Momentarily, Greg wondered himself. Was it parked?—moving? He grinned drunkenly. It gave him a feeling of power to know something about that car that even its owner didn't know: namely, that, in eight days, at two-sixteen on a Thursday afternoon, it would run down a little boy and kill him.

He focused his eyes and glared at Carrie. "All right, say it," he demanded. "Get it out."

She turned and looked at him imploringly. "Does it have to be so much?" she asked.

He turned his face away from her and closed his eyes.

"Greg, does it—"

"*Yes!*" He drew in a shaking breath. God, would he be glad to get away from her!

"What if they can't pay?"

"*Tough.*"

The sound of her repressed sob set his teeth on edge. "Go in and lie down," he told her.

"Greg, he hasn't got a chance!"

He twisted around, face whitening. "Did he have a better chance before we came?" he snarled. "Use your head for once, God damn it! If it wasn't for us, he'd be as good as dead already!"

"Yes, but—"

"I said go in and lie down!"

"You haven't seen the way it's going to happen, Greg!"

He shuddered violently, fighting back the urge to grab the whiskey bottle, leap at her and smash her head in. "*Get out of here*," he muttered.

She stumbled across the room, pressing the back of a hand against her lips. The bedroom door thumped shut and he heard her fall across the bed, sobbing. Damn wet-eye bitch! He gritted his teeth until his jaws hurt, then poured himself another inch of whiskey, grimacing as it burned its way into his stomach. They'll come through, he told himself. Obviously, they had the money and, obviously, the woman had believed him. He nodded to himself. They'll come through, all right. Ten thousand; his passport to another life. Expensive clothes. A class hotel. Good-looking women; maybe one of them for keeps. He kept nodding. One of these days, he thought.

He was reaching for his glass when he heard the muffled sound of Carrie talking in the bedroom. For several moments, his outstretched hand hovered between the sofa and the table. Then, in an instant, he was on his feet, lunging for the bedroom door. He flung it open. Carrie jerked around, the phone receiver in her hand, her face a mask of dread. "Thursday, the fourteenth!" she blurted into the mouthpiece. "Two-sixteen in the afternoon!" She screamed as Greg wrenched the receiver from her hand and slammed his palm on the cradle, breaking the connection.

He stood quivering before her, staring at her face with widened, maniac eyes. Slowly, Carrie raised her hand to avert the blow. "Greg, please don't—" she began.

Fury deafened him. He couldn't hear the heavy, thudding sound the earpiece made against her cheek as he slammed it

across her face with all his might. She fell back with a strangled cry. "You bitch," he gasped. "You bitch, you bitch, you
bitch!" He emphasized each repetition of the word with another savage blow across her face. He couldn't see her clearly
either; she kept wavering behind a film of blinding rage.
Everything was finished! She'd blown the deal! The Big
One was gone! *God damn it, I'll kill you!* He wasn't certain if
the words exploded in his mind or if he was shouting them
into her face.

Abruptly, he became aware of the telephone receiver
clutched in his aching hand; of Carrie lying, open-mouthed
and staring on the bed, her features mashed and bloody. He
lost his grip and heard, as if it were a hundred miles below,
the receiver thumping on the floor. He stared at Carrie, sick
with horror. Was she dead? He pressed his ear against her
chest and listened. At first, he could hear only the pulse of
his own heart throbbing in his ears. Then, as he concen-
trated, his expression tautly rabid, he became aware of Carrie's heartbeat, faint and staggering. She wasn't dead! He
jerked his head up.

She was looking at him, mouth slack, eyes dumbly stark.
"Carrie?"

No reply. Her lips moved soundlessly. She kept on staring at him. "What?" he asked. He recognized the look and
shuddered. "*What?*"

"Street," she whispered.

Greg bent over, staring at her mangled features. "Street,"
she whispered, ". . . night." She sucked in wheezing, blood-
choked breath. "Greg." She tried to sit up but couldn't. Her

expression was becoming one of terrified concern. She whispered, "Man . . . razor . . . you—oh, *no!*"

Greg felt himself enveloped in ice. He clutched at her arm. "Where?" he mumbled. She didn't answer and his fingers dug convulsively into her flesh. "Where?" he demanded. "When?" He began to shiver uncontrollably. "Carrie, *when?!*"

It was the arm of a dead woman that he clutched. With a gagging sound, he jerked his hand away. He gaped at her, unable to speak or think. Then, as he backed away, his eyes were drawn to the calendar on the wall and a phrase crept leadenly across his mind: *one of these days.* Quite suddenly, he began to laugh and cry. And before he fled, he stood at the window for an hour and twenty minutes, staring out, wondering who the man was, where he was right now and just what he was doing.

DYING ROOM ONLY

The cafe was a rectangle of brick and wood with an attached shed on the edge of the little town. They drove past it at first and started out into the heat-shimmering desert.

Then Bob said, "Maybe we'd better stop there. Lord knows how far it is to the next one."

"I suppose," Jean said without enthusiasm.

"I know it's probably a joint," Bob said, "but we have to eat something. It's been more than five hours since we had breakfast."

"Oh—all right."

Bob pulled over to the side of the road and looked back. There wasn't another car in sight. He made a quick U-turn and powered the Ford back along the road, then turned in and braked in front of the cafe.

"Boy, I'm starved," he said.

"So am I," Jean said. "I was starved last night, too, until the waitress brought that food to the table."

Bob shrugged. "So what can we do?" he said. "Is it better we starve and they find our bleached bones in the desert?"

She made a face at him and they got out of the car. "Bleached bones," she said.

The heat fell over them like a waterfall as they stepped into the sun. They hurried toward the cafe, feeling the burning ground through their sandals.

"It's so hot," Jean said, and Bob grunted.

The screen door made a groaning sound as they pulled it open. Then it slapped shut behind them and they were in the stuffy interior that smelled of grease and hot dust.

The three men in the cafe looked up at them as they entered. One, in overalls and a dirty cap, sat slumped in a back booth drinking beer. Another sat on a counter stool, a sandwich in his hand and a bottle of beer in front of him. The third man was behind the counter looking at them over a lowered newspaper. He was dressed in a white, short-sleeved shirt and wrinkled white ducks.

"Here we go," Bob whispered to her. "The Ritz-Carleton."

She enunciated slowly, "Ha-ha."

They moved to the counter and sat down on stools. The three men still looked at them.

"Our arrival in town must be an event," Bob said softly.

"We're celebrities," Jean said.

The man in the white ducks came over and drew a menu from behind a tarnished napkin holder. He slid it across the counter toward them. Bob opened it up and the two of them looked at it.

"Have you got any iced tea?" Bob asked.

The man shook his head. "No."

"Lemonade?" Jean asked.

The man shook his head. They looked at the menu again.

"What have you got that's cold?" Bob asked.

"Hi-Li Orange and Dr Pepper," said the man in a bored voice.

Bob cleared his throat.

"May we have some water before we order? We've been—"

The man turned away and walked back to the sink. He ran water into two cloudy glasses and brought them back. They spilled over onto the counter as he set them down. Jean picked up her glass and took a sip. She almost choked on the water it was so brackish and warm. She put down the glass.

"Can't you get it any cooler?" she asked.

"This is desert country, ma'am," he said. "We're lucky we get any water at all."

He was a man in his early fifties, his hair steel-gray and dry, parted in the middle. The backs of his hands were covered with tiny swirls of black hair, and on the small finger of his right hand there was a ring with a red stone in it. He stared at them with lifeless eyes and waited for their order.

"I'll have a fried egg sandwich on rye toast and—" Bob started.

"No toast," said the man.

"All right, plain rye then."

"No rye."

Bob looked up. "What kind of bread have you got?" he asked.

"White."

Bob shrugged. "White then. And a strawberry malted. How about you, honey?"

The man's flat gaze moved over to Jean.

"I don't know," she said. She looked up at the man. "I'll decide while you're making my husband's order."

The man looked at her a moment longer, then turned away and walked back to the stove.

"This is awful," Jean said.

"I know, honey," Bob admitted, "but what can we do? We don't know how far it is to the next town."

Jean pushed away the cloudy glass and slid off the stool.

"I'm going to wash up," she said. "Maybe then I'll feel more like eating."

"Good idea," he said.

After a moment, he got off his stool, too, and walked to the front of the cafe where the two restrooms were.

His hand was on the doorknob when the man eating at the counter called, "Think it's locked, mister."

Bob pushed.

"No it isn't," he said and went in.

Jean came out of the washroom and walked back to her stool at the counter. Bob wasn't there. He must be washing up, too, she thought. The man who had been eating at the counter was gone.

The man in the white ducks left his small gas stove and came over.

"You want to order now?" he asked.

"What? Oh." She picked up the menu and looked at it for a moment. "I'll have the same thing, I guess."

The man went back to the stove and broke another egg on the edge of the black pan. Jean listened to the sound of the eggs frying. She wished Bob would come back. It was unpleasant sitting there alone in the hot, dingy cafe.

Unconsciously she picked up the glass of water again and took a sip. She grimaced at the taste and put down the glass.

A minute passed. She noticed that the man in the back booth was looking at her. Her throat contracted and the fingers of her right hand began drumming slowly on the counter. She felt her stomach muscles drawing in. Her right hand twitched suddenly as a fly settled on it.

Then she heard the door to the men's washroom open, and she turned quickly with a sense of body-lightening relief.

She shuddered in the hot cafe.

It wasn't Bob.

She felt her heart throbbing unnaturally as she watched the man return to his place at the counter and pick up his unfinished sandwich. She averted her eyes as he glanced at her. Then, impulsively, she got off the stool and went back to the front of the cafe.

She pretended to look at a rack of sunfaded postcards, but her eyes kept moving to the brownish-yellow door with the word MEN painted on it.

Another minute passed. She saw that her hands were starting to shake. A long breath trembled her body as she looked in nervous impatience at the door.

She saw the man in the back booth push himself up and plod slowly down the length of the cafe. His cap was pushed to the back of his head and his high-topped shoes clomped heavily on the floor boards. Jean stood rigidly, holding a postcard in her hands as the man passed her. The washroom door opened and closed behind him.

Silence. Jean stood there staring at the door, trying to hold herself under control. Her throat moved again. She took a deep breath and put the postcard back in place.

"Here's your sandwich," the man at the counter called.

Jean started at the sound of his voice. She nodded once at him but stayed where she was.

Her breath caught as the washroom door opened again. She started forward instinctively, then drew back as the other man walked out, his face florid and sweaty. He started past her.

"Pardon me," she said.

The man kept moving. Jean hurried after him and touched his arm, her fingers twitching at the feel of the hot, damp cloth.

"Excuse me," she said.

The man turned and looked at her with dull eyes. His breath made her stomach turn.

"Did you see my—my husband in there?"

"Huh?"

Her hands closed into fists at her sides.

"Was my husband in the washroom?"

He looked at her a moment as if he didn't understand her. Then he said, "No, ma'am," and turned away.

It was very hot in there, but Jean felt as if she'd suddenly been submerged in a pool of ice water. She stood numbly watching the man stumble back to his booth.

Then she found herself hurrying for the counter, for the man who sat drinking from his water-beaded bottle of beer.

He put down the bottle and turned to face her as she came up.

"Pardon me, but did you see my husband in the washroom before?"

"Your husband?"

She bit her lower lip. "Yes, my husband. You saw him when we came in. Wasn't he in the washroom when you were there?"

"I don't recollect as he was, ma'am."

"You mean you didn't see him in there?"

"I don't recollect seein' him, ma'am."

"Oh this—this is ridiculous," she burst out in angry fright. "He must have been in there."

For a moment they stood looking at each other. The man didn't speak; his face was blank.

"You're—sure?" she asked.

"Ma'am, I got no reason to lie to you."

"All right. Thank you."

She sat stiffly at the counter staring at the two sandwiches and milk shakes, her mind in desperate search of a solution. It was Bob—he was playing a joke on her. But he wasn't in the habit of playing jokes on her and this was certainly no place to start. Yet he must have. There must be another door to the washroom and—

Of course. It wasn't a joke. Bob hadn't gone into the washroom at all. He'd just decided that she was right; the place was awful and he'd gone out to the car to wait for her.

She felt like a fool as she hurried toward the door. The man might have told her that Bob had gone out. Wait till she told Bob what she'd done. It was really funny how a person could get upset over nothing.

As she pulled open the screen door she wondered if Bob had paid for what they'd ordered. He must have. At least the man didn't call after her as she went out.

She moved into the sunlight and started toward the car, almost closing her eyes completely to shut out the glare on the windshield. She smiled to herself thinking about her foolish worrying.

"Bob, wait till I—"

Unreasoning dread pressed her insides into a tight knot. She stood in the pounding heat and stared into the empty car. She felt a scream pushing up in her throat. "*Bob*—"

She started running around the side of the cafe looking for the other entrance. Maybe the washroom was too dirty; maybe Bob had gone out a side door and couldn't find his way around the shed that was attached to the cafe.

She tried to look through one of the shed's windows, but it was covered with tar paper on the inside. She ran around to the back of the cafe and looked out across the wide, empty desert. Then she turned back and looked for footprints, but the ground was as hard as baked enamel. A whimper started in her throat and she knew that in a few seconds she was going to start crying.

"Bob," she murmured. "Bob, where—?"

In the stillness she heard the front screen door slap in its frame. Abruptly she started running up the side of the cafe building, heart hammering excitedly. Stifling heat waves broke over her as she ran.

At the edge of the building she stopped suddenly.

The man she'd spoken to at the counter was looking into the car. He was a small man in his forties, wearing a spotted fedora and a striped, green shirt. Black suspenders held up his dark, grease-spotted pants. Like the other man he wore high-top shoes.

She moved one step and her sandal scuffed on the dry ground. The man looked over at her suddenly, his face lean and bearded. His eyes were a pale blue that shone like milk spots in the leathery tan of his face.

The man smiled casually. "Thought I'd see if your husband was waitin' on you in your car," he said. He touched the brim of his hat and started back into the cafe.

"Are you—" Jean started, then broke off as the man turned.

"Ma'am?"

"Are you sure he wasn't in the washroom?"

"Wasn't no one in there when I went in," he said.

She stood shivering in the sun as the man went into the cafe and the screen door flapped closed. She could feel mindless dread filling her like ice water.

Then she caught herself. There had to be an explanation. Things like this just didn't happen.

She moved firmly across the cafe floor and stopped before

the counter. The man in the white ducks looked up from his paper.

"Would you please check the washroom?" she asked.

"The washroom?"

Anger tightened her.

"Yes, the washroom," she said. "I know my husband is in there."

"Ma'am, wasn't no one in there," said the man in the fedora.

"I'm sorry," she said tightly, refusing to allow his words. "My husband didn't just disappear."

The two men made her nervous with their silent stares.

"Well, are you going to look there?" she said, unable to control the break in her voice.

The man in the white ducks glanced at the man with the fedora and something twitched his mouth. Jean felt her hands jerk into angry fists. Then he moved down the length of the counter and she followed.

He turned the porcelain knob and held open the spring-hinged door. Jean held her breath as she moved closer to look.

The washroom was empty.

"Are you satisfied?" the man said. He let the door swing shut.

"Wait," she said. "Let me look again."

The man pressed his mouth into a line.

"Didn't you see it was empty?" he said.

"I said I want to look again."

"Lady, I'm tellin' ya—"

Jean pushed at the door suddenly and it banged against the washroom wall.

"There!" she said. "There's a door there!"

She pointed to a door in the far wall of the washroom.

"That door's been locked for years, lady," the man said.

"It doesn't open?"

"Ain't got no reason to open it."

"It must open," Jean said. "My husband went in there and he didn't come out this door. And he didn't disappear!"

The man looked at her sullenly without speaking.

"What's on the other side of the door?" she asked.

"Nothing."

"Does it open on the outside?"

The man didn't answer.

"Does it?!"

"It opens on a shed, lady, a shed no one's used for years," the man said angrily.

She stepped forward and gripped the knob of the door.

"I told you it didn't open." The man's voice was rising more.

"Ma'am?" Behind her Jean heard the cajoling voice of the man in the fedora and green shirt. "Ain't nothin' in that shed but old trash, ma'am. You want, I'll show it to you."

The way he said it, Jean suddenly realized that she was alone. Nobody she knew knew where she was; there was no way of checking if—

She moved out of the washroom quickly.

"Excuse me," she said as she walked by the man in the fedora, "I want to make a call first."

She walked stiffly to the wall phone, shuddering as she thought of them coming after her. She picked up the ear piece. There was no dial tone. She waited a moment, then tensed herself and turned to face the two watching men.

"Does—does it work?"

"Who ya call—" started the man in the white ducks, but the other man interrupted.

"You gotta crank it, ma'am," he said slowly. Jean noticed the other man glaring at him suddenly, and when she turned back to the phone, she heard their voices whispering heatedly.

She turned the crank with shaking fingers. *What if they come at me?* The thought wouldn't leave her.

"Yes?" a thin voice asked over the phone.

Jean swallowed. "Would you get me the marshal, please?" she asked.

"Marshal?"

"Yes, the—"

She lowered her voice suddenly, hoping the men wouldn't hear her. "The *marshal*," she repeated.

"There's no marshal, ma'am."

She felt close to screaming. "Who do I call?"

"You might want the sheriff, ma'am," the operator said.

Jean closed her eyes and ran her tongue over dry lips. "The sheriff then," she said.

There was a sputtering sound over the phone, a series of dull buzzes and then the sound of a receiver being lifted.

"Sheriff's office," said a voice.

"Sheriff, would you please come out to—"

"One second. I'll get the sheriff."

Jean's stomach muscles pulled in and her throat became taut. As she waited, she felt the eyes of the two men on her. She heard one of them move and her shoulders twitched spasmodically.

"Sheriff speaking."

"Sheriff, would you please come out to the—"

Her lips trembled as she realized suddenly that she didn't know the name of the cafe. She turned nervously and her heartbeat lurched when she saw the men looking at her coldly.

"What's the name of the cafe?"

"Why do you want to know?" asked the man in the white ducks.

He isn't going to tell me, she thought. *He's going to make me go out to look at the sign so that he can*—

"Are you going to—" she started to say, then turned quickly as the sheriff said, "Hello?"

"Please don't hang up," she said hurriedly. "I'm in a cafe on the edge of the town near the desert. On the western edge of town, I mean. I came here with my husband and now he's gone. He—just disappeared."

The sound of her own words made her shudder.

"You at the Blue Eagle?" the sheriff asked.

"I—I don't know," she said. "I don't know the name. They won't tell—"

Again she broke off nervously.

"Ma'am, if you want to know the name," said the man in the fedora, "it's the Blue Eagle."

"Yes, yes," she relayed to the mouthpiece. "The Blue Eagle."

"I'll be right over," said the sheriff.

"What you tell her for?" the man in the white ducks spoke angrily behind her.

"Son, we don't want no trouble with the sheriff. We ain't done nothin'. Why shouldn't he come?"

For a long moment Jean leaned her forehead against the phone and drew in deep breaths. *They can't do anything now,* she kept telling herself. *I've told the sheriff and they have to leave me alone.* She heard one of the men moving to the door but no sound of the door opening.

She turned and saw that the man in the fedora was looking out the door while the other one stared at her.

"You tryin' to make trouble for my place?" he asked.

"I'm not trying to make trouble, but I want my husband back."

"Lady, we ain't done nothing with your husband!"

The man in the fedora turned around with a wry grin. "Looks like your husband lit out," he said blandly.

"He did not!" Jean said angrily.

"Then where's your car, ma'am?" the man asked.

There was a sudden dropping sensation in her stomach. Jean ran to the screen door and pushed out.

The car was gone.

"Bob!"

"Looks like he left you behind, ma'am," said the man.

She looked at the man with frightened eyes, then turned away with a sob and stumbled across the porch. She stood there in the oven-hot shade crying and looking at the place where the car had been. The dust was still settling there.

She was still standing on the porch when the dusty blue patrol car braked in front of the cafe. The door opened and a tall, red-haired man got out, dressed in gray shirt and trousers, with a dull, metallic star pinned over his heart. Jean moved numbly off the porch to meet him.

"You the lady that called?" the man asked.

"Yes, I am."

"What's wrong now?"

"I told you. My husband disappeared."

"Disappeared?"

As quickly as possible she told him what had happened.

"You don't think he drove away then?" said the sheriff.

"He wouldn't leave me here like this."

The sheriff nodded. "All right, go on," he said.

When she was finished, the sheriff nodded again and they went inside. They went to the counter.

"This lady's husband go in the lavatory, Jim?" the sheriff asked the man in the white ducks.

"How should I know?" the man asked. "I was cooking. Ask Tom, he was in there." He nodded toward the man in the fedora.

"What about it, Tom?" asked the sheriff.

"Sheriff, didn't the lady tell you her husband just lit out before in their car?"

"That's not true!" Jean cried.

"You see the man driving the car away, Tom?" the sheriff asked.

"Sure I saw him. Why else would I say it?"

"No. No." Jean murmured the word with tiny, frightened shakes of her head.

"Why didn't you call after him if you saw him?" the sheriff asked Tom.

"Sheriff, ain't none of my business if a man wants to run out on—"

"He didn't run out!"

The man in the fedora shrugged his shoulders with a grin. The sheriff turned to Jean.

"Did you see your husband go in the lavatory?"

"Yes, of course I—well, no, I didn't exactly see him go in, but—"

She broke off into angry silence as the man in the fedora chuckled.

"I know he went in," she said, "because after I came out of the ladies washroom I went outside and the car was empty. Where else could he have been? The cafe is only so big. There's a door in that washroom. He said it hasn't been used in years." She pointed at the man in the white ducks. "But I know it has. I know my husband didn't just leave me here. He wouldn't do it. I know him, and he wouldn't do it!"

"Sheriff," said the man in white ducks, "I showed the washroom to her when she asked. There wasn't nobody in there and she can't say there was."

Jean twisted her shoulders irritably.

"He went through that other door," she said.

"Lady, that door ain't used!" the man said loudly. Jean flinched and stepped back.

"All right, take it easy, Jim," the sheriff said. "Lady, if you didn't see your husband go in that lavatory and you didn't see if it was somebody else drivin' your car away, I don't see what we got to go on."

"What?"

She couldn't believe what she'd heard. Was the man actually telling her there was nothing to be done? For a second she tightened in fury thinking that the sheriff was just sticking up for his own townspeople against a stranger. Then the impact of being alone and helpless struck her and her breath caught as she looked at the sheriff with childlike, frightened eyes.

"Lady, I don't see what I can do," the sheriff said with a shake of his head.

"Can't you—" She gestured timidly. "Can't you l-look in the washroom for a clue or something? Can't you open that door?"

The sheriff looked at her for a moment, then pursed his lips and walked down to the washroom. Jean followed him closely, afraid to stay near the two men.

She looked into the washroom as the sheriff was testing the closed door. She shuddered as the man in the white ducks came down and stood beside her.

"I told her it don't open," he said to the sheriff. "It's locked on the other side. How could the man get out?"

"Someone might have opened it on the other side," Jean said nervously.

The man made a sound of disgust.

"Anyone else been around here?" the sheriff asked Jim.

"Just Sam McComas havin' some beer before, but he went home about—"

"I mean in this shed."

"Sheriff, you know there ain't."

"What about big Lou?" the sheriff asked.

Jim was quiet a second and Jean saw his throat move.

"He ain't been around for months, Sheriff," Jim said. "He went up north."

"Jim, you better go around and open up this door," the sheriff said.

"Sheriff, ain't nothin' but an empty shed in there."

"I know, Jim, I know. Just want to satisfy the lady."

Jean stood there feeling the looseness around her eyes again, the sick feeling of being without help. It made her dizzy, as if everything were spinning away from her. She held one fist with her other hand and all her fingers were white.

Jim went out the screen door with a disgusted mutter and the door slapped shut behind him.

"Lady, come here," Jean heard the sheriff say quickly and softly. Her heart jumped as she moved into the washroom.

"You recognize this?"

She looked at the shred of cloth in his palm, then she gasped, "That's the color slacks he had on!"

"Ma'am, not so loud," the sheriff said. "I don't want them to think I know anything."

He stepped out of the washroom suddenly as he heard boots on the floor. "You goin' somewhere, Tom?" he asked.

"No, no, Sheriff," said the man in the fedora. "Just comin' down to see how you was gettin' on."

"Uh-huh. Well—stick around for a while, will you, Tom?" said the sheriff.

"Sure, Sheriff, sure," Tom said broadly. "I ain't goin' nowhere."

They heard a clicking sound in the washroom, and in a moment the door was pulled open. The sheriff walked past Jean and down three steps into a dimly lit shed.

"Got a light in here?" he asked Jim.

"Nope, ain't got no reason to. No one ever uses it."

The sheriff pulled a light string, but nothing happened.

"Don't you believe me, Sheriff?" Jim said.

"Sure I do, Jim," said the sheriff. "I'm just curious."

Jean stood in the doorway looking down into the damp-smelling shed.

"Kinda beat up in here," said the sheriff, looking at a knocked-over table and chair.

"No one's been here for years, Sheriff," Jim said. "Ain't no reason to tidy it up."

"Years, eh?" the sheriff said half to himself as he moved around the shed. Jean watched him, her hands numb at the fingertips, shaking. Why didn't he find out where Bob was? That shred of cloth—how did it get torn from Bob's slacks? She gritted her teeth hard. *I mustn't cry*, she ordered herself. *I just mustn't cry. I know he's all right. He's perfectly all right.*

The sheriff stopped and bent over to pick up a newspaper. He glanced at it casually, then folded it and hit it against one palm casually.

"Years, eh?" he said.

"Well, I haven't been here in years," Jim said hurriedly,

licking his lips. "Could be that—oh, Lou or somebody been holin' up in here sometime the last year. I don't keep the outside door locked ya know."

"Thought you said Lou went up north," the sheriff said mildly.

"He did, he did. I say in the last year he might have—"

"This is yesterday's paper, Jim," the sheriff said.

Jim looked blank, started to say something and then closed his mouth without making a sound. Jean felt herself trembling without control now. She didn't hear the screen door close quietly in front of the cafe or the furtive footsteps across the porch boards.

"Well—I didn't say Lou was the only one who might have sneaked in here for a night," Jim said quickly. "Could have been any tramp passing by."

He stopped as the sheriff looked around suddenly, his gaze darting past Jean. "Where's Tom?" he asked loudly.

Jean's head snapped around. Then she backed away with a gasp as the sheriff dashed up the steps and ran by her.

"Stick around, Jim!" the sheriff called over his shoulder.

Jean rushed out of the cafe after him. As she came out on the porch she saw the sheriff shading his eyes with one hand and looking up the road. Her eyes jumped in the same direction, and she saw the man in the fedora running toward another man, a tall man.

"That'd be Lou," she heard the sheriff murmur to himself.

He started running; then, after a few steps, he came back and jumped into his car.

"Sheriff!"

He glanced out the window and saw the look of fright on her face. "All right, hurry up! Get in!"

She jumped off the porch and ran toward the car. The sheriff pushed open the door and Jean slid in beside him and pulled it shut. The sheriff gunned his car out past the cafe and it skidded onto the road in a cloud of dust.

"What is it?" Jean asked him breathlessly.

"Your husband didn't leave you," was all the sheriff said.

"Where is he?" she asked in a frightened voice.

But they were already overtaking the two men who had met and were now running into the brush.

The sheriff jerked the car off the road and slammed on the brakes. He pushed out of the car, quickly reaching down for his pistol.

"Tom!" he yelled. "Lou! Stop running!"

The men kept going. The sheriff leveled his pistol barrel and fired. Jean started at the explosion and saw, far out across the rocky desert, a spout of sand jump up near the men.

They both stopped abruptly, turned and held up their hands.

"Come on back!" yelled the sheriff. "And make it fast!"

Jean stood beside the car, unable to keep her hands from shaking. Her eyes were fastened on the two men walking toward them.

"All right, where is he?" the sheriff asked as they came up.

"Who you talkin' about, Sheriff?" asked the man in the fedora.

"Never mind that, Tom," the sheriff said angrily. "I'm

not foolin' anymore. This lady wants her husband back. Now where—"

"Husband!" Lou looked at the man in the fedora with angry eyes. "I thought we decided agin that!"

"Shut your mouth!" the man in the fedora said, his pleasant demeanor gone entirely now.

"You told me we wasn't gonna—" Lou started.

"Let's see what you got in your pockets, Lou," the sheriff said.

Lou looked at the sheriff blankly. "My pockets?" he said.

"Come on, come on." The sheriff waved his pistol impatiently. Lou started emptying his pockets slowly.

"Told me we wasn't gonna do that," he muttered aside to the man in the fedora. "Told me. Stupid jackass."

Jean gasped as Lou tossed the wallet on the ground. "That's Bob's," she murmured.

"Get his things, lady," the sheriff said.

Nervously she moved over at the feet of the men and picked up the wallet, the coins, the car keys.

"All right, where is he?" the sheriff asked. "And don't waste my time!" he said angrily to the man in the fedora.

"Sheriff, I don't know what you—" started the man.

The sheriff almost lunged forward. "So help me!" he raged. Tom threw up one arm and stepped back.

"I'll tell you for a fact, Sheriff," Lou broke in. "If I'd known this fella had his woman with him, I'd never've done it."

Jean stared at the tall, ugly man, her teeth digging into her lower lip. *Bob, Bob.* Her mind kept saying his name.

"Where is he, I said," the sheriff demanded.

"I'll show you, I'll show you," Lou said. "I told you I never would've done it if I'd known his woman was with him."

Again he turned to the man in the fedora. "Why'd you let him go in there?" he demanded. "Why? Answer me that?"

"Don't know what he's talkin' about, Sheriff," Tom said blandly. "Why, I—"

"Get on the road," the sheriff ordered. "Both of you. You take us to him or you're really in trouble. I'm followin' you in the car. Don't make any wrong move, not one."

The car moved slowly behind the two walking men.

"I been after these boys for a year," the sheriff told her. "They set themselves up a nice little system robbin' men who come to the cafe, then dumpin' them in the desert and sellin' their car up north."

Jean hardly heard what he was saying. She kept staring at the road ahead, her stomach tight, her hands pressed tightly together.

"Never knew how they worked it though," the sheriff went on. "Never thought of the lavatory. Guess what they did was keep it locked for any man but one who was alone. They must've slipped up today. I guess Lou just jumped anyone who came in there. He's not any too bright."

"Do you think they—" Jean started hesitantly.

The sheriff hesitated. "I don't know, lady. I wouldn't think so. They ain't that dumb. Besides we had cases like this before and they never hurt no one worse than a bump on the head."

He honked the horn. "Come on, snap it up!" he called to the men.

"Are there snakes out there?" Jean asked.

The sheriff didn't answer. He just pressed his mouth together and stepped on the accelerator so the men had to break into a trot to keep ahead of the bumper.

A few hundred yards further on, Lou turned off and started down a dirt road.

"Oh my God, where did they take him?" Jean asked.

"Should be right down here," the sheriff said.

Then Lou pointed to a clump of trees and Jean saw their car. The sheriff stopped his coupe and they got out. "All right, where is he?" he asked.

Lou started across the broken desert ground. Jean kept feeling the need to break into a run. She had to tense herself to keep walking by the sheriff's side. Their shoes crunched over the dry desert soil. She hardly felt the pebbles through her sandals, so intently was she studying the ground ahead.

"Ma'am," Lou said, "I hope you won't be too hard on me. If I'd known you was with him, I'd've never touched him."

"Knock it off, Lou," the sheriff said. "You're both in up to your necks, so you might as well save your breath."

Then Jean saw the body lying out on the sand, and with a sob she ran past the men, her heart pounding.

"Bob—"

She held his head in her lap, and when his eyes fluttered open, she felt as if the earth had been taken off her back.

He tried to smile, then winced at the pain. "I been hit," he muttered.

Without a word, the tears came running down her cheeks. She helped him back to their car, and as she followed the sheriff's car, she held tightly to Bob's hand all the way back to town.

A FLOURISH OF STRUMPETS

One evening in October the doorbell rang.

Frank and Sylvia Gussett had just settled down to watch television. Frank put his gin and tonic on the table and stood. He walked into the hall and opened the door.

It was a woman.

"Good evening," she said. "I represent the Exchange."

"The Exchange?" Frank smiled politely.

"Yes," said the woman. "We're beginning an experimental program in this neighborhood. As to our service—"

Their service was a venerable one. Frank gaped.

"Are you *serious*?" he asked.

"Perfectly," the woman said.

"But—good Lord, you can't—come to our very houses and—and—that's against the law! I can have you arrested!"

"Oh, you wouldn't want to do *that*," said the woman. She absorbed blouse-enhancing air.

"Oh, wouldn't I?" said Frank and closed the door in her face.

He stood there breathing hard. Outside, he heard the sound of the woman's spike heels clacking down the porch steps and fading off.

Frank stumbled into the living room.

"It's unbelievable," he said.

Sylvia looked up from the television set. "What is?" she asked.

He told her.

"*What!*" She rose from her chair, aghast.

They stood looking at each other a moment. Then Sylvia strode to the phone and picked up the receiver. She spun the dial and told the operator, "*I want the police.*"

"Strange business," said the policeman who arrived a few minutes later.

"Strange indeed," mused Frank.

"Well, what are you going to *do* about it?" challenged Sylvia.

"Not much we *can* do right off, ma'am," explained the policeman. "Nothing to go on."

"But my description—" said Frank.

"We can't go around arresting every woman we see in spike heels and a white blouse," said the policeman. "If she comes back, you let us know. Probably just a sorority prank, though."

"Perhaps he's right," said Frank when the patrol car had driven off.

Sylvia replied, "He'd better be."

Strangest thing happened last night," said Frank to Maxwell as they drove to work.

Maxwell snickered. "Yeah, she came to our house, too," he said.

"She did?" Frank glanced over, startled, at his grinning neighbor.

"Yeah," said Maxwell. "Just my luck the old lady had to answer the door."

Frank stiffened. "*We* called the police," he said.

"What for?" asked Maxwell. "Why fight it?"

Frank's brow furrowed. "You mean you—don't think it was a sorority girl prank?" he asked.

"Hell, no, man," said Maxwell, "it's for real." He began to sing:

> *I'm just a poor little*
> > *door-to-door whore;*
> *A want-to-be-good*
> *But misunderstood . . .*

"What on earth?" asked Frank.

"Heard it at a stag party," said Maxwell. "Guess this isn't the first town they've hit."

"*Good Lord*," muttered Frank, blanching.

"Why not?" asked Maxwell. "It was just a matter of time. Why should they let all that home trade go to waste?"

"That's *execrable*," declared Frank.

"Hell it is," said Maxwell. "It's progress."

The second one came that night; a black-root blonde, slit-skirted and sweatered to within an inch of her breathing life.

"*Hel*-lo, honey," she said when Frank opened the door. "The name's Janie. Interested?"

Frank stood rigid to the heels. "I—" he said.

"Twenty-three and fancy free," said Janie.

Frank shut the door, quivering.

"*Again?*" asked Sylvia as he tottered back.

"Yes," he mumbled.

"Did you get her address and phone number so we can tell the police?"

"I forgot," he said.

"Oh!" Sylvia stamped her mule. "You said you were going to."

"I know." Frank swallowed. "Her name was—Janie."

"That's a *big* help," Sylvia said. She shivered. "*Now* what are we going to do?"

Frank shook his head.

"Oh, this is *monstrous,*" she said. "That we should be exposed to such—" She trembled with fury.

Frank embraced her. "Courage," he whispered.

"I'll get a dog," she said. "A vicious one."

"No, no," he said, "we'll call the police again. They'll simply have to station someone out here."

Sylvia began to cry. "It's monstrous," she sobbed, "that's all."

"Monstrous," he agreed.

W hat's that you're humming?" she asked at breakfast.

He almost spewed out whole wheat toast.

"Nothing," he said, choking. "Just a song I heard."

She patted him on the back. "Oh."

He left the house, mildly shaken. It *is* monstrous, he thought.

That morning, Sylvia bought a sign at a hardware store and hammered it into the front lawn. It read NO SOLICITING. She underlined the SOLICITING. Later she went out again and underlined the underline.

Came right to your door, you say?" asked the FBI man Frank phoned from the office.

"*Right to the door,*" repeated Frank, "bold as you please."

"My, my," said the FBI man. He clucked.

"Notwithstanding," said Frank sternly, "the police have refused to station a man in our neighborhood."

"I see," said the FBI man.

"Something has got to be done," declared Frank. "This is a gross invasion of privacy."

"It certainly is," said the FBI man, "and we will look into the matter, never fear."

After Frank had hung up, he returned to his bacon sandwich and thermos of buttermilk.

"*I'm just a poor little—*" he had sung before catching himself. Shocked, he totted figures the remainder of his lunch hour.

The next night it was a perky brunette with a blouse front slashed to forever.

"No!" said Frank in a ringing voice.

She wiggled sumptuously. "Why?" she asked.

"*I do not have to explain myself to you!*" he said and shut the door, heart pistoning against his chest.

Then he snapped his fingers and opened the door again. The brunette turned, smiling.

"Changed your mind, honey?" she asked.

"No. I mean *yes*," said Frank, eyes narrowing. "What's your address?"

The brunette looked mildly accusing.

"Now, honey," she said. "You wouldn't be trying to get me in trouble, would you?"

"She wouldn't tell me," he said dismally when he returned to the living room.

Sylvia looked despairing. "I phoned the police again," she said.

"And—?"

"And *nothing*. There's the smell of corruption in this."

Frank nodded gravely. "You'd better get that dog," he said. He thought of the brunette. "A *big* one," he added.

W owee, that Janie," said Maxwell.

Frank downshifted vigorously and yawed around a corner on squealing tires. His face was adamantine.

Maxwell clapped him on the shoulder.

"Aw, come off it, Frankie-boy," he said, "you're not fooling me any. You're no different from the rest of us."

"I'll have no part in it," declared Frank, "and that's all there is to it."

"So keep telling that to the Mrs.," said Maxwell. "But get in a few kicks on the side like the rest of us. Right?"

"Wrong," said Frank. "*All* wrong. No *wonder* the police can't do anything. I'm probably the only willing witness in town."

Maxwell guffawed.

It was a raven-haired, limp-lidded vamp that night. On

her outfit spangles moved and glittered at strategic points.

"Hel-*lo,* honey lamb," she said. "My name's—"

"*What have you done with our dog?*" challenged Frank.

"Why, nothing, honey, nothing," she said. "He's just off getting acquainted with my poodle Winifred. Now about *us*—"

Frank shut the door without a word and waited until the twitching had eased before returning to Sylvia and television.

Semper, by God oh God, he thought as he put on his pajamas later, *fidelis.*

The next two nights they sat in the darkened living room and, as soon as the woman rang the doorbell, Sylvia phoned the police.

"*Yes,*" she whispered, furiously, "they're right out there *now.* Will you please send a patrol car *this instant?*"

Both nights the patrol car arrived after the women had gone.

"Complicity," muttered Sylvia as she daubed on cold cream. "Plain out-and-out complicity."

Frank ran cold water over his wrists.

That day Frank phoned city and state officials who promised to look into the matter.

That night it was a redhead sheathed in a green knit dress that hugged all that was voluminous and there was much of that.

"Now, see here—" Frank began.

"Girls who were here before me," said the redhead, "tell

me you're not interested. Well, I always say, where there's a disinterested husband there's a listening wife."

"Now you see here—" said Frank.

He stopped as the redhead handed him a card. He looked at it automatically.

39-26-36

MARGIE

(SPECIALTIES)

BY APPOINTMENT ONLY.

"If you don't want to set it up here, honey," said Margie, "you just meet me in the Cyprian Room of the Hotel Fillmore."

"I *beg* your pardon," said Frank and flung the card away.

"Any evening between six and seven," Margie chirped.

Frank leaned against the shut door and birds with heated wings buffeted at his face.

"Monstrous," he said with a gulp. "Oh, m-*monstrous*."

"*Again?*" asked Sylvia.

"But with a difference," he said vengefully. "I have traced them to their lair and tomorrow I shall lead the police there."

"Oh, Frank!" said Sylvia, embracing him. "You're wonderful."

"Th-thank you," said Frank.

When he came out of the house the next morning he found the card on one of the porch steps. He picked it up and slid it into his wallet.

Sylvia mustn't see it, he thought.

It would hurt her.

Besides, he had to keep the porch neat.

Besides, it was important evidence.

That evening he sat in a shadowy Cyprian Room booth revolving a glass of sherry between two fingers. Jukebox music softly thrummed; there was the mumble of post-work conversation in the air.

Now, thought Frank. *When Margie arrives, I'll duck into the phone booth and call the police, then keep her occupied in conversation until they come. That's what I'll do. When Margie—*

Margie arrived.

Frank sat like a Medusa victim. Only his mouth moved. It opened slowly. His gaze rooted on the jutting opulence of Margie as she waggled along the aisle, then came to gelatinous rest on a leather-topped bar stool.

Five minutes later he cringed out of a side door.

"Wasn't *there?*" asked Sylvia for a third time.

"I *told* you," snapped Frank, concentrating on his breaded cutlet.

Sylvia was still a moment. Then her fork clinked down.

"We'll have to move, then," she said. "Obviously, the authorities have no intention of doing *anything.*"

"What difference does it make *where* we live?" he mumbled.

She didn't reply.

"I mean," he said, trying to break the painful silence, "well, who knows, maybe it's an inevitable cultural phenomenon. Maybe—"

"*Frank Gussett!*" she cried. "*Are you defending that awful Exchange?*"

"No, no, of course not," he blurted. "It's execrable. Really! But—well, maybe it's Greece all over again. Maybe it's Rome. Maybe it's—"

"I don't care *what* it is!" she cried. "It's *awful!*"

He put his hand on hers. "There, there," he said. *39-26-36,* he thought.

That night, in the frantic dark, there was a desperate reaffirmation of their love.

"It *was* nice, *wasn't* it?" asked Sylvia, plaintively.

"Of course," he said. *39-26-36.*

That's right!" said Maxwell as they drove to work the next morning. "A cultural phenomenon. You hit it on the head, Frankie boy. An inevitable goddamn cultural phenomenon. First the houses. Then the lady cab drivers, the girls on street corners, the clubs, the teenage pickups roaming the drive-in movies. Sooner or later they had to branch out more; put it on a door-to-door basis. And naturally, the syndicates are going to run it, pay off complainers. Inevitable. You're so right, Frankie boy; so right."

Frank drove on, nodding grimly.

Over lunch he found himself humming, "*Mar-gie. I'm always thinkin' of you—*"

He stopped, shaken. He couldn't finish the meal. He prowled the streets until one, marble-eyed. The mass mind, he thought, that evil old mass mind.

Before he went into his office he tore the little card to confetti and snowed it into a disposal can.

In the figures he wrote that afternoon the number 39 cropped up with dismaying regularity.

Once with an exclamation point.

I almost think you *are* defending this—this *thing*," accused Sylvia. "You and your cultural phenomenons!"

Frank sat in the living room listening to her bang dishes in the kitchen sink. Cranky old thing, he thought.

MARGIE

(*specialties*)

Will you stop! he whispered furiously to his mind.

That night while he was brushing his teeth, he started to sing, "*I'm just a poor little—*"

"Damn!" he muttered to his wild-eyed reflection.

That night there were dreams. Unusual ones.

The next day he and Sylvia argued.

The next day Maxwell told him his system.

The next day Frank muttered to himself more than once, "I'm so tired of it all."

The next night the women stopped coming.

"Is it *possible*?" said Sylvia. "Are they actually going to leave us alone?"

Frank held her close. "Looks like it," he said faintly. *Oh, I'm despicable,* he thought.

A week went by. No women came. Frank woke daily at six a.m. and did a little dusting and vacuuming before he left for work.

"I like to help you," he said when Sylvia asked. She looked at him strangely. When he brought home bouquets three nights in a row she put them in water with a quizzical look on her face.

It was the following Wednesday night.

The doorbell rang. Frank stiffened. They'd *promised* to stop coming!

"I'll get it," he said.

"Do," she said.

He clumped to the door and opened it.

"Evening, sir."

Frank stared at the handsome, mustached young man in the jaunty sports clothes.

"I'm from the Exchange," the man said. "Wife home?"

NO SUCH THING AS A VAMPIRE

In the early autumn of the year 18—Madame Alexis Gheria awoke one morning to a sense of utmost torpor. For more than a minute, she lay inertly on her back, her dark eyes staring upward. How wasted she felt. It seemed as if her limbs were sheathed in lead. Perhaps she was ill, Petre must examine her and see.

Drawing in a faint breath, she pressed up slowly on an elbow. As she did, her nightdress slid, rustling, to her waist. How had it come unfastened? she wondered, looking down at herself.

Quite suddenly, Madame Gheria began to scream.

In the breakfast room, Dr. Petre Gheria looked up, startled, from his morning paper. In an instant, he had pushed his chair back, slung his napkin on the table and was rushing for the hallway. He dashed across its carpeted breadth and mounted the staircase two steps at a time.

It was a near hysterical Madame Gheria he found sitting on the edge of her bed looking down in horror at her breasts. Across the dilated whiteness of them, a smear of blood lay drying.

Dr. Gheria dismissed the upstairs maid, who stood frozen in the open doorway, gaping at her mistress. He locked the door and hurried to his wife.

"Petre!" she gasped.

"Gently." He helped her lie back across the blood-stained pillow.

"Petre, what *is* it?" she begged.

"Lie still, my dear." His practiced hands moved in swift search over her breasts. Suddenly, his breath choked off. Pressing aside her head, he stared down dumbly at the pin-prick lancinations on her neck, the ribbon of tacky blood that twisted downward from them.

"My *throat*," Alexis said.

"No, it's just a—" Dr. Gheria did not complete the sentence. He knew exactly what it was.

Madame Gheria began to tremble. "Oh, my God, my *God*," she said.

Dr. Gheria rose and foundered to the washbasin. Pouring in water, he returned to his wife and washed away the blood. The wound was clearly visible now—two tiny punctures close to the jugular. A grimacing Dr. Gheria touched the mounds of inflamed tissue in which they lay. As he did, his wife groaned terribly and turned her face away.

"Now listen to me," he said, his voice apparently calm. "We will not succumb, immediately, to superstition, do you hear? There are any number of—"

"I'm going to die," she said.

"Alexis, do you hear me?" He caught her harshly by the shoulders.

She turned her head and stared at him with vacant eyes. "You know what it is," she said.

Dr. Gheria swallowed. He could still taste coffee in his mouth.

"I know what it appears to be," he said, "and we shall— not ignore the possibility. However—"

"I'm going to die," she said.

"Alexis!" Dr. Gheria took her hand and gripped it fiercely. "*You shall not be taken from me,*" he said.

Solta was a village of some thousand inhabitants situated in the foothills of Rumania's Bihor Mountains. It was a place of dark traditions. People, hearing the bay of distant wolves, would cross themselves without a thought. Children would gather garlic buds as other children gather flowers, bringing them home for the windows. On every door there was a painted cross, at every throat a metal one. Dread of the vampire's blighting was as normal as the dread of fatal sickness. It was always in the air.

Dr. Gheria thought about that as he bolted shut the windows of Alexis' room. Far off, molten twilight hung above the mountains. Soon it would be dark again. Soon the citizens of Solta would be barricaded in their garlic-reeking houses. He had no doubt that every soul of them knew exactly what had happened to his wife. Already the cook and upstairs maid were pleading for discharge. Only the inflexible discipline of the butler, Karel, kept them at their jobs. Soon, even that would not suffice. Before the horror of the vampire, reason fled.

He'd seen the evidence of it that very morning when he'd ordered Madame's room stripped to the walls and searched for rodents or venomous insects. The servants had moved about the room as if on a floor of eggs, their eyes more white than pupil, their fingers twitching constantly to their crosses. They had known full well no rodent or insects would be found. And Gheria had known it. Still, he'd raged at them for their timidity, succeeding only in frightening them further.

He turned from the window with a smile.

"There now," said he, "nothing alive will enter this room tonight."

He caught himself immediately, seeing the flare of terror in her eyes.

"Nothing at *all* will enter," he amended.

Alexis lay motionless on her bed, one pale hand at her breast, clutching at the worn silver cross she'd taken from her jewel box. She hadn't worn it since he'd given her the diamond-studded one when they were married. How typical of her village background that, in this moment of dread, she should seek protection from the unadorned cross of her church. She was such a child. Gheria smiled down gently at her.

"You won't be needing that, my dear," he said, "you'll be safe tonight."

Her fingers tightened on the crucifix.

"No, no, wear it if you will," he said. "I only meant that I'll be at your side all night."

"You'll stay with me?"

He sat on the bed and held her hand.

"Do you think I'd leave you for a moment?" he said.

Thirty minutes later, she was sleeping. Dr. Gheria drew a chair beside the bed and seated himself. Removing his glasses, he massaged the bridge of his nose with the thumb and forefinger of his left hand. Then, sighing, he began to watch his wife. How incredibly beautiful she was. Dr. Gheria's breath grew strained.

"There is no such thing as a vampire," he whispered to himself.

There was a distant pounding. Dr. Gheria muttered in his sleep, his fingers twitching. The pounding increased; an agitated voice came swirling from the darkness. "Doctor!" it called.

Gheria snapped awake. For a moment, he looked confusedly towards the locked door.

"Dr. Gheria?" demanded Karel.

"What?"

"Is everything all right?"

"Yes, everything is—"

Dr. Gheria cried out hoarsely, springing for the bed. Alexis' nightdress had been torn away again. A hideous dew of blood covered her chest and neck.

Karel shook his head.

"Bolted windows cannot hold away the creature, sir," he said.

He stood, tall and lean, beside the kitchen table on which lay the cluster of silver he'd been polishing when Gheria had entered.

"The creature has the power to make itself a vapor which can pass through any opening, however small," he said.

"But the cross!" cried Gheria. "It was still at her throat—untouched! Except by—blood," he added in a sickened voice.

"This I cannot understand," said Karel, grimly. "The cross should have protected her."

"But why did I see nothing?"

"You were drugged by its mephitic presence," Karel said. "Count yourself fortunate that you were not also attacked."

"I do not count myself fortunate!" Dr. Gheria struck his palm, a look of anguish on his face. "What am I to do, Karel?" he asked.

"Hang garlic," said the old man. "Hang it at the windows, at the doors. Let there be no opening unblocked by garlic."

Gheria nodded distractedly. "Never in my life have I seen this thing," he said, brokenly. "Now, my own wife—"

"I have seen it," said Karel. "I have, myself, put to its rest one of these monsters from the grave."

"The stake—?" Gheria looked revolted.

The old man nodded slowly.

Gheria swallowed. "Pray God you may put this one to rest as well," he said.

Petre?"

She was weaker now, her voice a toneless murmur. Gheria bent over her. "Yes, my dear," he said.

"It will come again tonight," she said.

"No." He shook his head determinedly. "It cannot come. The garlic will repel it."

NO SUCH THING AS A VAMPIRE   91

"My cross didn't," she said, "you didn't."

"The garlic will," he said. "And see?" He pointed at the bedside table. "I've had black coffee brought for me. I won't sleep tonight."

She closed her eyes, a look of pain across her sallow features.

"I don't want to die," she said. "Please don't let me die, Petre."

"You won't," he said. "I promise you; the monster shall be destroyed."

Alexis shuddered feebly. "But if there is no way, Petre," she murmured.

"There is always a way," he answered.

Outside the darkness, cold and heavy, pressed around the house. Dr. Gheria took his place beside the bed and began to wait. Within the hour, Alexis slipped into a heavy slumber. Gently, Dr. Gheria released her hand and poured himself a cup of steaming coffee. As he sipped it hotly, bitter, he looked around the room. Door locked, windows bolted, every opening sealed with garlic, the cross at Alexis' throat. He nodded slowly to himself. It will work, he thought. The monster would be thwarted.

He sat there, waiting, listening to his breath.

Dr. Gheria was at the door before the second knock.

"Michael!" He embraced the younger man. "Dear Michael, I was sure you'd come!"

Anxiously, he ushered Dr. Vares towards his study. Outside darkness was just falling.

"Where on earth are all the people of the village?" asked Vares. "I swear, I didn't see a soul as I rode in."

"Huddling, terror-stricken, in their houses," Gheria said, "and all my servants with them save for one."

"Who is that?"

"My butler, Karel," Gheria answered. "He didn't answer the door because he's sleeping. Poor fellow, he is very old and has been doing the work of five." He gripped Vares' arm. "Dear Michael," he said, "you have no idea how glad I am to see you."

Vares looked at him worriedly. "I came as soon as I received your message," he said.

"And I appreciate it," Gheria said. "I know how long and hard a ride it is from Cluj."

"What's wrong?" asked Vares. "Your letter only said—"

Quickly, Gheria told him what had happened in the past week.

"I tell you, Michael, I stumble at the brink of madness," he said. "Nothing works! Garlic, wolfsbane, crosses, mirrors, running water—useless! No, don't say it! This isn't superstition nor imagination! This is *happening*! A vampire is destroying her! Each day she sinks yet deeper into that—deadly torpor from which—"

Gheria clinched his hands. "And yet I cannot understand it."

"Come, sit, sit." Doctor Vares pressed the older man into a chair, grimacing at the pallor of him. Nervously, his fingers sought for Gheria's pulse beat.

"Never mind me," protested Gheria. "It's Alexis we must

help." He pressed a sudden, trembling hand across his eyes. "Yet how?" he said.

He made no resistance as the younger man undid his collar and examined his neck.

"You, too," said Vares, sickened.

"What does that matter?" Gheria clutched at the younger man's hand. "My friend, my dearest friend," he said, "tell me that it is not I! Do *I* do this hideous thing to her?"

Vares looked confounded. "*You?*" he said. "But—"

"I know, I know," said Gheria. "I, myself, have been attacked. Yet nothing follows, Michael! What breed of horror is this which cannot be impeded? From what unholy place does it emerge? I've had the countryside examined foot by foot, every graveyard ransacked, every crypt inspected! There is no house within the village that has not yet been subjected to my search. I tell you, Michael, there is nothing! Yet, there *is* something—something which assaults us nightly, draining us of life. The village is engulfed by terror—and I as well! I never see this creature, never hear it! Yet, every morning, I find my beloved wife—"

Vares's face was drawn and pallid now. He stared intently at the older man.

"What am I to do, my friend?" pleaded Gheria. "How am I to save her?"

Vares had no answer.

How long has she—been like this?" asked Vares. He could not remove his stricken gaze from the whiteness of Alexis' face.

"For many days," said Gheria. "The retrogression has been constant."

Dr. Vares put down Alexis' flaccid hand. "Why did you not tell me sooner?" he asked.

"I thought the matter could be handled," Gheria answered, faintly. "I know now that it—cannot."

Vares shuddered. "But, surely—" he began.

"There is nothing left to be done," said Gheria. "Everything has been tried, *everything*!" He stumbled to the window and stared out bleakly into the deepening night. "And now it comes again," he murmured, "and we are helpless before it."

"Not helpless, Petre." Vares forced a cheering smile to his lips and laid his hand upon the older man's shoulder. "I will watch her tonight."

"It's useless."

"Not at all, my friend," said Vares, nervously. "And now you must sleep."

"I will not leave her," said Gheria.

"But you need rest."

"I cannot leave," said Gheria. "I will not be separated from her."

Vares nodded. "Of course," he said. "We will share the hours of watching then."

Gheria sighed. "We can try," he said, but there was no sound of hope in his voice.

Some twenty minutes later, he returned with an urn of steaming coffee which was barely possible to smell through the heavy mist of garlic fumes which hung in the air. Trudging to the bed, Gheria set down the tray. Dr. Vares had drawn a chair up beside the bed.

"I'll watch first," he said. "You sleep, Petre."

"It would do no good to try," said Gheria. He held a cup beneath the spigot and the coffee gurgled out like smoking ebony.

"Thank you," murmured Vares as the cup was handed to him. Gheria nodded once and drew himself a cupful before he sat.

"I do not know what will happen to Solta if this creature is not destroyed," he said. "The people are paralyzed by terror."

"Has it—been elsewhere in the village?" Vares asked him.

Gheria sighed exhaustedly. "Why need it go elsewhere?" he said. "It is finding all it—craves within these walls." He stared despondently at Alexis. "When we are gone," he said, "it will go elsewhere. The people know that and are waiting for it."

Vares set down his cup and rubbed his eyes.

"It seems impossible," he said, "that we, practitioners of a science, should be unable to—"

"What can science effect against it?" said Gheria. "Science which will not even admit its existence? We could bring, into this very room, the foremost scientists of the world and they would say—my friends, you have been deluded. There is no vampire. All is mere trickery."

Gheria stopped and looked intently at the younger man. He said, "Michael?"

Vares's breath was slow and heavy. Putting down his cup of untouched coffee, Gheria stood and moved to where Vares sat slumped in his chair. He pressed back an eyelid, looked down briefly at the sightless pupil, then withdrew his hand. The drug was quick, he thought. And most effective. Vares would be insensible for more than time enough.

Moving to the closet, Gheria drew down his bag and carried it to the bed. He tore Alexis's nightdress from her upper body and, within seconds, had drawn another syringe full of her blood; this would be the last withdrawal, fortunately. Staunching the wound, he took the syringe to Vares and emptied it into the young man's mouth, smearing it across his lips and teeth.

That done, he strode to the door and unlocked it. Returning to Vares, he raised and carried him into the hall. Karel would not awaken; a small amount of opiate in his food had seen to that. Gheria labored down the steps beneath the weight of Vares's body. In the darkest corner of the cellar, a wooden casket waited for the younger man. There he would lie until the following morning when the distraught Dr. Petre Gheria would, with sudden inspiration, order Karel to search the attic and cellar on the remote, nay fantastic possibility that—

Ten minutes later, Gheria was back in the bedroom checking Alexis's pulse beat. It was active enough; she would survive. The pain and torturing horror she had undergone would be punishment enough for her. As for Vares—

Dr. Gheria smiled in pleasure for the first time since

Alexis and he had returned from Cluj at the end of the summer. Dear spirits in heaven, would it not be sheer enchantment to watch old Karel drive a stake through Michael Vares's damned cuckolding heart!

PATTERN FOR SURVIVAL

And they stood beneath the crystal towers, beneath the polished heights which, like scintillant mirrors, caught rosy sunset on their faces until their city was one vivid, coruscated blush.

Ras slipped an arm about the waist of his beloved.

"Happy?" he inquired, in a tender voice.

"Oh, yes," she breathed. "Here in our beautiful city where there is peace and happiness for all, how could I be anything but happy?"

Sunset cast its roseate benediction upon their soft embrace.

THE END

The clatter ceased. His hands curled in like blossoms and his eyes fell shut. The prose was wine. It trickled on the taste buds of his mind, a dizzying potion. I've done it again, he recognized, by George in heaven, I've done it again.

Satisfaction towed him out to sea. He went down for the third time beneath its happy drag. Surfacing then, reborn, he estimated wordage, addressed envelope, slid in manuscript, weighed total, affixed stamps and sealed. Another brief submergence in the waters of delight, then up withal and to the mailbox.

It was almost twelve as Richard Allen Shaggley hobbled down the quiet street in his shabby overcoat. He had to hurry or he'd miss the pickup and he mustn't do that. *Ras and the City of Crystal* was too superlative to wait another day. He wanted it to reach the editor immediately. It was a certain sale.

Circuiting the giant, pipe-strewn hole (When, in the name of heaven would they finish repairing that blasted sewer?), he limped on hurriedly, envelope clutched in rigid fingers, heart a turmoil of vibration.

Noon. He reached the mailbox and cast about anxious glances for the postman. No sign of him. A sigh of pleasure and relief escaped his chapped lips. Face aglow, Richard Allen Shaggley listened to the envelope thump gently on the bottom of the mailbox.

The happy author shuffled off, coughing.

Al's legs were bothering him again. He shambled up the quiet street, teeth gritted slightly, leather sack pulling down his weary shoulder. Getting old, he thought, haven't got the drive any more. Rheumatism in the legs. Bad; makes it hard to do the route.

At twelve-fifteen, he reached the dark green mailbox and drew the keys from his pocket. Stooping, with a groan, he opened up the box and drew out its contents.

A smiling eased his pain-tensed face; he nodded once. Another yarn by Shaggley. Probably be snatched up right away. The man could really write.

Rising with a grunt, Al slid the envelope into his sack, relocked the mailbox, then trudged off, still smiling to himself. Makes a man proud, he thought, carrying his stories; even if my legs do hurt.

Al was a Shaggley fan.

W hen Rick arrived from lunch a little after three that afternoon, there was a note from his secretary on the desk.

New ms. from Shaggley just arrived, it read. *Beautiful job. Don't forget R.A. wants to see it when you're through. S.*

Delight cast illumination across the editor's hatchet face. By George in heaven, this was manna from what had threatened to be a fruitless afternoon. Lips drawn back in what, for him, was smiling, he dropped into his leather chair, restrained emphatic finger twitchings for the blue pencil (No need of it for a Shaggley yarn!) and plucked the envelope from the cracked glass surface of his desk. By George, a Shaggley story; what luck! R.A. would beam.

He sank into the cushion, instantly absorbed in the opening nuance of the tale. A tremor of transport palsied outer sense. Breathless, he plunged on into the story depths. *What balance, what delineation!* How the man could write. Distractedly, he brushed plaster dust off his pinstripe sleeve.

As he read, the wind picked up again, fluttering his straw-like hair, buffeting like tepid wings against his brow. Unconsciously, he raised his hand and traced a delicate finger along the scar which trailed like livid thread across his cheek and lower temple.

The wind grew stronger. It moaned by pretzeled I-beams and scattered brown-edged papers on the soggy

rug. Rick stirred restlessly and stabbed a glance at the gaping
fissure in the wall (When, in the name of heaven, would
they finish those repairs?), then returned, joy renewed, to
Shaggley's manuscript.

Finishing at last, he fingered away a tear of bittersweetness and depressed an intercom key.

"Another check for Shaggley," he ordered, then tossed
the snapped-off key across his shoulder.

At three-thirty, he brought the manuscript to R.A.'s office and left it there.

At four, the publisher laughed and cried over it, gnarled
fingers rubbing at the scabrous bald patch on his head.

Old hunchbacked Dick Allen set type for Shaggley's story
that very afternoon, vision blurred by happy tears beneath
his eyeshade, liquid coughing unheard above the busy clatter
of his machine.

The story hit the stand a little after six. The scar-faced
dealer shifted on his tired legs as he read it over six times before, reluctantly, offering it for sale.

At half past six, the little bald-patched man came hobbling down the street. A hard day's work, a well-earned rest,
he thought, stopping at the corner newsstand for some reading matter.

He gasped. By George in heaven, a new Shaggley story!
What luck!

The only copy, too. He left a quarter for the dealer who
wasn't there at the moment.

He took the story home, shambling by skeletal ruins

(strange, those burned buildings hadn't been replaced yet), reading as he went.

He finished the story before arriving home. Over supper, he read it once again, shaking his lumpy head at the marvel of its impact, the unbreakable magic of its workmanship. It inspires, he thought.

But not tonight. Now was the time for putting things away: the cover on the typewriter, the shabby overcoat, threadbare pinstripe, eyeshade, mailman's cap and leather sack all in their proper places.

He was asleep by ten, dreaming about mushrooms. And, in the morning, wondering once again why those first observers had not described the cloud as more like a toadstool.

By six a.m. Shaggley, breakfasted, was at the typewriter.

This is the story, he wrote, *of how Ras met the beautiful priestess of Shahglee and she fell in love with him.*

MUTE

The man in the dark raincoat arrived in German Corners at two-thirty that Friday afternoon. He walked across the bus station to a counter behind which a plump, gray-haired woman was polishing glasses.

"Please," he said, "where might I find authority?"

The woman peered through rimless glasses at him. She saw a man in his late thirties, a tall, good-looking man.

"Authority?" she asked.

"Yes—how do you say it? The constable? The—?"

"Sheriff?"

"Ah." The man smiled. "Of course. The sheriff. Where might I find him?"

After being directed, he walked out of the building into the overcast day. The threat of rain had been constant since he'd woken up that morning as the bus was pulling over the mountains into Casca Valley. The man drew up his collar, then slid both hands into the pockets of his raincoat and started briskly down Main Street.

Really, he felt tremendously guilty for not having come sooner; but there was so much to do, so many problems to overcome with his own two children. Even knowing that something was wrong with Holger and Fanny, he'd been unable to get away from Germany until now—almost a year since they'd last heard from the Nielsens. It was a shame that Holger had chosen such an out-of-the-way place for his corner of the four-sided experiment.

Professor Werner walked more quickly, anxious to find out what had happened to the Nielsens and their son. Their progress with the boy had been phenomenal—really an inspiration to them all. Although Werner felt, deep within himself, that something terrible had happened, he hoped they were all alive and well. Yet, if they were, how to account for the long silence?

Werner shook his head worriedly. Could it have been the town? Elkenberg had been compelled to move several times in order to avoid the endless prying—sometimes innocent, more often malicious—into *his* work. Something similar might have happened to Nielsen. The workings of the small town composite mind could, sometimes, be a terrible thing.

The sheriff's office was in the middle of the next block. Werner strode more quickly along the narrow sidewalk, then pushed open the door and entered the large, warmly heated room.

"Yes?" the sheriff asked, looking up from his desk.

"I have come to inquire about a family," Werner said, "the name of Nielsen."

Sheriff Harry Wheeler looked blankly at the tall man.

Cora was pressing Paul's trousers when the call came. Setting the iron on its stand, she walked across the kitchen and lifted the receiver from the wall telephone.

"Yes?" she said.

"Cora, it's me."

Her face tightened. "Is something wrong, Harry?"

He was silent.

"Harry?"

"The one from Germany is here."

Cora stood motionless, staring at the calendar on the wall, the numbers blurred before her eyes.

"Cora, did you hear me?"

She swallowed dryly. "Yes."

"I—I have to bring him out to the house," he said.

She closed her eyes.

"I know," she murmured and hung up.

Turning, she walked slowly to the window. It's going to rain, she thought. Nature was setting the scene well.

Abruptly, her eyes shut, her fingers drew in tautly, the nails digging at her palms.

"No." It was almost a gasp. "*No.*"

After a few moments she opened her tear-glistening eyes and looked out fixedly at the road. She stood there numbly, thinking of the day the boy had come to her.

If the house hadn't burned in the middle of the night there might have been a chance. It was twenty-one miles from German Corners but the state highway ran fifteen of them and the last six—the six miles of dirt road that led north into the wood-sloped hills—might have been navigated had there been more time.

As it happened, the house was a night-lashing sheet of flame before Bernhard Klaus saw it.

Klaus and his family lived some five miles away on Sky-touch Hill. He had gotten out of bed around one-thirty to get a drink of water. The window of the bathroom faced north and that was why, entering, Klaus saw the tiny flaring blaze out in the darkness.

"*Gott'n'immel!*" He slung startled words together and was out of the room before he'd finished. He thumped heavily down the carpeted steps, then, feeling at the wall for guidance, hurried for the living room.

"Fire at Nielsen house!" he gasped after agitated cranking had roused the night operator from her nap.

The hour, the remoteness, and one more thing doomed the house. German Corners had no official fire brigade. The security of its brick and timbered dwellings depended on voluntary effort. In the town itself this posed no serious problem. It was different with those houses in the outlying areas.

By the time Sheriff Wheeler had gathered five men and driven them to the fire in the ancient truck, the house was lost. While four of the six men pumped futile streams of water into the leaping, crackling inferno, Sheriff Wheeler and his deputy, Max Ederman, circuited the house.

There was no way in. They stood in back, raised arms warding off the singeing buffet of heat, grimacing at the blaze.

"They're done for!" Ederman yelled above the windswept roar.

Sheriff Wheeler looked sick. "The *boy*," he said but Ederman didn't hear.

Only a waterfall could have doused the burning of the old house. All the six men could do was prevent ignition of the woods that fringed the clearing. Their silent figures prowled the edges of the glowing aura, stamping out sparks, hosing out the occasional flare of bushes and tree foliage.

They found the boy just as the eastern hill peaks were being edged with gray morning.

Sheriff Wheeler was trying to get close enough to see into one of the side windows when he heard a shout. Turning, he ran towards the thick woods that sloped downwards a few dozen yards behind the house. Before he'd reached the underbrush, Tom Poulter emerged from them, his thin frame staggering beneath the weight of Paal Nielsen.

"Where'd you find him?" Wheeler asked, grabbing the boy's legs to ease weight from the older man's back.

"Down the hill," Poulter gasped. "Lyin' on the ground."

"Is he burned?"

"Don't look it. His pajamas ain't touched."

"Give him here," the sheriff said. He shifted Paal into his own strong arms and found two large, green-pupilled eyes staring blankly at him.

"You're awake," he said, surprised.

The boy kept staring at him without making a sound.

"You all right, son?" Wheeler asked. It might have been a statue he held, Paal's body was so inert, his expression so dumbly static.

"Let's get a blanket on him," the sheriff muttered aside and started for the truck. As he walked he noticed how the boy stared at the burning house now, a look of masklike rigidity on his face.

"*Shock,*" murmured Poulter and the sheriff nodded grimly.

They tried to put him down on the cab seat, a blanket over him but he kept sitting up, never speaking. The coffee Wheeler tried to give him dribbled from his lips and across his chin. The two men stood beside the truck while Paal stared through the windshield at the burning house.

"Bad off," said Poulter. "Can't talk, cry, nor nothing."

"He isn't burned," Wheeler said, perplexed. "How'd he get out of the house without getting burned?"

"Maybe his folks got out, too," said Poulter.

"Where are they then?"

The older man shook his head. "Dunno, Harry."

"Well, I better take him home to Cora," the sheriff said. "Can't leave him sitting out here."

"Think I'd better go with you," Poulter said. "I have t'get the mail sorted for delivery."

"All right."

Wheeler told the other four men he'd bring back food and replacements in an hour or so. Then Poulter and he climbed into the cab beside Paal and he jabbed his boot toe on the starter. The engine coughed spasmodically, groaned over, then caught. The sheriff raced it until it was warm, then eased it into gear. The truck rolled off slowly down the dirt road that led to the highway.

Until the burning house was no longer visible, Paal stared out the back window, face still immobile. Then, slowly, he turned, the blanket slipping off his thin shoulders. Tom Poulter put it back over him.

"Warm enough?" he asked.

The silent boy looked at Poulter as if he'd never heard a human voice in his life.

As soon as she heard the truck turn off the road, Cora Wheeler's quick right hand moved along the stove-front switches. Before her husband's bootfalls sounded on the back porch steps, the bacon lay neatly in strips across the frying pan, white moons of pancake batter were browning on the griddle, and the already-brewed coffee was heating.

"Harry."

There was a sound of pitying distress in her voice as she saw the boy in his arms. She hurried across the kitchen.

"Let's get him to bed," Wheeler said. "I think maybe he's in shock."

The slender woman moved up the stairs on hurried feet, threw open the door of what had been David's room, and moved to the bed. When Wheeler passed through the doorway she had the covers peeled back and was plugging in an electric blanket.

"Is he hurt?" she asked.

"No." He put Paal down on the bed.

"Poor darling," she murmured, tucking in the bedclothes around the boy's frail body. "Poor little darling." She stroked back the soft blond hair from his forehead and smiled down at him.

"There now, go to sleep, dear. It's all right. Go to sleep."

Wheeler stood behind her and saw the seven-year-old boy staring up at Cora with that same dazed, lifeless expression. It hadn't changed once since Tom Poulter had brought him out of the woods.

The sheriff turned and went down to the kitchen. There he phoned for replacements, then turned the pancakes and bacon, and poured himself a cup of coffee. He was drinking it when Cora came down the back stairs and returned to the stove.

"Are his parents—?" she began.

"I don't know," Wheeler said, shaking his head. "We couldn't get near the house."

"But the boy—?"

"Tom Poulter found him outside."

"Outside."

"We don't know how he got out," he said. "All we know's he was there."

His wife grew silent. She slid pancakes on a dish and put the dish in front of him. She put her hand on his shoulder.

"You look tired," she said. "Can you go to bed?"

"Later," he said.

She nodded, then, patting his shoulder, turned away. "The bacon will be done directly," she said.

He grunted. Then, as he poured maple syrup over the stack of cakes, he said, "I expect they are dead, Cora. It's an awful fire; still going when I left. Nothing we could do about it."

"That poor boy," she said.

She stood by the stove watching her husband eat wearily.

"I tried to get him to talk," she said, shaking her head, "but he never said a word."

"Never said a word to us either," he told her, "just stared."

He looked at the table, chewing thoughtfully.

"Like he doesn't even know how to talk," he said.

A little after ten that morning the waterfall came—a waterfall of rain—and the burning house sputtered and hissed into charred, smoke-fogged ruins.

Red-eyed and exhausted, Sheriff Wheeler sat motionless in the truck cab until the deluge had slackened. Then, with a chest-deep groan, he pushed open the door and slid to the ground. There, he raised the collar of his slicker and pulled down the wide-brimmed Stetson more tightly on his skull. He walked around to the back of the covered truck.

"Come on," he said, his voice hoarsely dry. He trudged through the clinging mud towards the house.

The front door still stood. Wheeler and the other men bypassed it and clambered over the collapsed living room wall. The sheriff felt thin waves of heat from the still-glowing timbers and the throat-clogging reek of wet, smoldering rugs and upholstery turned his edgy stomach.

He stepped across some half-burned books on the floor and the roasted bindings crackled beneath his tread. He kept moving, into the hall, breathing through gritted teeth, rain spattering off his shoulders and back. I hope they got out, he thought, I hope to God they got out.

They hadn't. They were still in their bed, no longer human, blackened to a hideous, joint-twisted crisp. Sheriff

Wheeler's face was taut and pale as he looked down at them.

One of the men prodded a wet twig at something on the mattress.

"Pipe," Wheeler heard him say above the drum of rain. "Must have fell asleep smokin'."

"Get some blankets," Wheeler told them. "Put them in the back of the truck."

Two of the men turned away without a word and Wheeler heard them clump away over the rubble.

He was unable to take his eyes off Professor Holger Nielsen and his wife Fanny, scorched into grotesque mockeries of the handsome couple he remembered—the tall, big-framed Holger, calmly imperious; the slender, auburn-haired Fanny, her face a soft, rose-cheeked—

Abruptly, the sheriff turned and stumped from the room, almost tripping over a fallen beam.

The boy—what would happen to the boy now? That day was the first time Paal had ever left this house in his life. His parents were the fulcrum of his world; Wheeler knew that much. No wonder there had been that look of shocked incomprehension on Paal's face.

Yet how did he know his mother and father were dead?

As the sheriff crossed the living room, he saw one of the men looking at a partially charred book.

"Look at this," the man said, holding it out.

Wheeler glanced at it, his eyes catching the title: *The Unknown Mind.*

He turned away tensely. "Put it down!" he snapped, quitting the house with long, anxious strides. The memory of how the Nielsens looked went with him; and something else. A question.

How did Paal get out of the house?

Paal woke up.

For a long moment he stared up at the formless shadows that danced and fluttered across the ceiling. It was raining out. The wind was rustling tree boughs outside the window, causing shadow movements in this strange room. Paal lay motionless in the warm center of the bed, air crisp in his lungs, cold against his pale cheeks.

Where were they? Paal closed his eyes and tried to sense their presence. They weren't in the house. Where then? Where were his mother and father?

Hands of my mother. Paal washed his mind clean of all but the trigger symbol. They rested on the ebony velvet of his concentration—pale, lovely hands, soft to touch and be touched by, the mechanism that could raise his mind to the needed level of clarity.

In his own home it would be unnecessary. His own home was filled with the sense of them. Each object touched by them possessed a power to bring their minds close. The very air seemed charged with their consciousness, filled with a constancy of attention.

Not here. He needed to lift himself above the alien drag of here.

Therefore, I am convinced that each child is born with this in-stinctive ability. Words given to him by his father appearing again like dew-jewelled spiderweb across the fingers of his mother's hands. He stripped it off. The hands were free again, stroking slowly at the darkness of his mental focus. His eyes were shut; a tracery of lines and ridges scarred his brow, his tightened jaw was bloodless. The level of aware- ness, like waters, rose.

His senses rose along, unbidden.

Sound revealed its woven maze—the rushing, thudding, drumming, dripping rain; the tangled knit of winds through air and tree and gabled eave; the crackling settle of the house; each whispering transience of process.

Sense of smell expanded to a cloud of brain-filling odors—wood and wool, damp brick and dust and sweet starched linens. Beneath his tensing fingers weave became apparent—coolness and warmth, the weight of covers, the delicate, skin-scarring press of rumpled sheet. In his mouth the taste of cold air, old house. Of sight, only the hands.

Silence; lack of response. He'd never had to wait so long for answers before. Usually, they flooded on him easily. His mother's hands grew clearer. They pulsed with life. Un- known, he climbed beyond. *This bottom level sets the stage for more important phenomena.* Words of his father. He'd never gone above that bottom level until now.

Up, up. Like cool hands drawing him to rarified heights. Tendrils of acute consciousness rose towards the peak, searching desperately for a holding place. The hands began breaking into clouds. The clouds dispersed.

It seemed he floated towards the blackened tangle of his home, rain a glistening lace before his eyes. He saw the front door standing, waiting for his hand. The house drew closer. It was engulfed in licking mists. Closer, closer—

Paal, no.

His body shuddered on the bed. Ice frosted his brain. The house fled suddenly, bearing with itself a horrid image of two black figures lying on—

Paal jolted up, staring and rigid. Awareness maelstromed into its hiding place. One thing alone remained. He knew that they were gone. He knew that they had guided him, sleeping, from the house.

Even as they burned.

That night they knew he couldn't speak.

There was no reason for it, they thought. His tongue was there, his throat looked healthy. Wheeler looked into his opened mouth and saw that. But Paal did not speak.

"So *that*'s what it was," the sheriff said, shaking his head gravely. It was near eleven. Paal was asleep again.

"What's that, Harry?" asked Cora, brushing her dark blond hair in front of the dressing table mirror.

"Those times when Miss Frank and I tried to get the Nielsens to start the boy in school." He hung his pants across the chair back. "The answer was always no. Now I see why."

She glanced up at his reflection. "There must be something wrong with him, Harry," she said.

"Well, we can have Doc Steiger look at him but I don't think so."

"But they were college people," she argued. "There was no earthly reason why they shouldn't teach him how to talk. Unless there was some reason he *couldn't*."

Wheeler shook his head again.

"They were strange people, Cora," he said. "Hardly

spoke a word themselves. As if they were too good for talking—or something." He grunted disgustedly. "No wonder they didn't want that boy to school."

He sank down on the bed with a groan and shucked off boots and calf-high stockings. "What a day," he muttered.

"You didn't find anything at the house?"

"Nothing. No identification papers at all. The house is burned to a cinder. Nothing but a pile of books and they don't lead us anywhere."

"Isn't there any way?"

"The Nielsens never had a charge account in town. And they weren't even citizens so the professor wasn't registered for the draft."

"Oh." Cora looked a moment at her face reflected in the oval mirror. Then her gaze lowered to the photograph on the dressing table—David as he was when he was nine. The Nielsen boy looked a great deal like David, she thought. Same height and build. Maybe David's hair had been a trifle darker but—

"What's to be done with him?" she asked.

"Couldn't say, Cora," he answered. "We have to wait till the end of the month, I guess. Tom Poulter says the Nielsens got three letters the end of every month. Come from Europe, he said. We'll just have to wait for them, then write back to the addresses on them. May be the boy has relations over there."

"Europe," she said, almost to herself. "That far away."

Her husband grunted, then pulled the covers back and sank down heavily on the mattress.

"Tired," he muttered.

He stared at the ceiling. "Come to bed," he said.

"In a little while."

She sat there brushing distractedly at her hair until the sound of his snoring broke the silence. Then, quietly, she rose and moved across the hall.

There was a river of moonlight across the bed. It flowed over Paal's small, motionless hands. Cora stood in the shadows a long time looking at the hands. For a moment she thought it was David in his bed again.

It was the sound.

Like endless club strokes across his vivid mind, it pulsed and throbbed into him in an endless, garbled din. He sensed it was communication of a sort but it hurt his ears and chained awareness and locked incoming thoughts behind dense, impassable walls.

Sometimes, in an infrequent moment of silence he would sense a fissure in the walls and, for that fleeting moment, catch hold of fragments—like an animal snatching scraps of food before the trap jaws clash together.

But then the sound would start again, rising and falling in rhythmless beat, jarring and grating, rubbing at the live, glistening surface of comprehension until it was dry and aching and confused.

"Paal," she said.

A week had passed; another week would pass before the letters came.

"Paal, didn't they ever talk to you? Paal?"

Fists striking at delicate acuteness. Hands squeezing sensitivity from the vibrant ganglia of his mind.

"Paal, don't you know your name? Paal? *Paal*."

There was nothing physically wrong with him. Doctor Steiger had made sure of it. There was no reason for him not to talk.

"We'll teach you, Paal. It's all right, darling. We'll teach you." Like knife strokes across the weave of consciousness. "*Paal. Paal*."

Paal. It was himself; he sensed that much. But it was different in the ears, a dead, depressive sound standing alone and drab, without the host of linked associations that existed in his mind. In thought, his name was more than letters. It was *him,* every facet of his person and its meaning to himself, his mother and his father, to his life. When they had summoned him or thought his name it had been more than just the small hard core which sound made of it. It had been everything interwoven in a flash of knowing, unhampered by sound.

"Paal, don't you understand? It's your name. Paal Nielsen. Don't you understand?"

Drumming, pounding at raw sensitivity. Paal. The sound kicking at him. *Paal. Paal.* Trying to dislodge his grip and fling him into the maw of sound.

"Paal. *Try,* Paal. Say it after me. Pa-al. *Pa-al.*"

Twisting away, he would run from her in panic and she would follow him to where he cowered by the bed of her son.

Then, for long moments, there would be peace. She would hold him in her arms and, as if she understood, would not speak. There would be stillness and no pounding clash of sound against his mind. She would stroke his hair and kiss away sobless tears. He would lie against the warmth of her, his mind, like a timid animal, emerging from its hiding place again—to sense a flow of understanding from this woman. Feeling that needed no sound.

Love—wordless, unencumbered, and beautiful.

Sheriff Wheeler was just leaving the house that morning when the phone rang. He stood in the front hallway, waiting until Cora picked it up.

"Harry!" he heard her call. "Are you gone yet?"

He came back into the kitchen and took the receiver from her. "Wheeler," he said into it.

"Tom Poulter, Harry," the postmaster said. "Them letters is in."

"Be right there," Wheeler said and hung up.

"The letters?" his wife asked.

Wheeler nodded.

"*Oh,*" she murmured so that he barely heard her.

When Wheeler entered the post office twenty minutes later, Poulter slid the three letters across the counter. The sheriff picked them up.

"Switzerland," he read the postmarks, "Sweden, Germany."

"That's the lot," Poulter said, "like always. On the thirtieth of the month."

"Can't open them, I suppose," Wheeler said.

"Y'know I'd say yes if I could, Harry," Poulter answered. "But law's law. You know that. I got t'send them back unopened. That's the law."

"All right." Wheeler took out his pen and copied down

the return addresses in his pad. He pushed the letters back. "Thanks."

When he got home at four that afternoon, Cora was in the front room with Paal. There was a look of confused emotion on Paal's face—a desire to please coupled with a frightened need to flee the disconcertion of sound. He sat beside her on the couch looking as if he were about to cry.

"Oh, *Paal*," she said as Wheeler entered. She put her arms around the trembling boy. "There's nothing to be afraid of, darling."

She saw her husband.

"What did they *do* to him?" she asked, unhappily.

He shook his head. "Don't know," he said. "He should have been put in school though."

"We can't very well put him in school when he's like *this*," she said.

"We can't put him anywhere till we see what's what," Wheeler said. "I'll write those people tonight."

In the silence, Paal felt a sudden burst of emotion in the woman and he looked up quickly at her stricken face.

Pain. He felt it pour from her like blood from a mortal wound.

And while they ate supper in an almost silence, Paal kept sensing tragic sadness in the woman. It seemed he heard sobbing in a distant place. As the silence continued he began to get momentary flashes of remembrance in her pain-opened mind. He saw the face of another boy. Only it swirled and faded and there was *his* face in her thoughts. The two faces, like contesting wraiths, lay and overlay upon each other as if fighting for the dominance of her mind.

All fleeing, locked abruptly behind black doors as she said, "You have to write to them, I suppose."

"You know I do, Cora," Wheeler said.

Silence. Pain again. And when she tucked him into bed, he looked at her with such soft, apparent pity on his face that she turned quickly from the bed and he could feel the waves of sorrow break across his mind until her footsteps could no longer be heard. And, even then, like the faint fluttering of bird wings in the night, he felt her pitiable despair moving in the house.

What are you writing?" she asked.

Wheeler looked over from his desk as midnight chimed its seventh stroke in the hall. Cora came walking across the room and set the tray down at his elbow. The steamy fragrance of freshly brewed coffee filled his nostrils as he reached for the pot.

"Just telling them the situation," he said, "about the fire, the Nielsens dying. Asking them if they're related to the boy or know any of his relations over there."

"And what if his relations don't do any better than his parents?"

"Now, Cora," he said, pouring cream, "I thought we'd already discussed that. It's not our business."

She pressed pale lips together.

"A frightened child *is* my business," she said angrily. "Maybe you—"

She broke off as he looked up at her patiently, no argument in his expression.

"*Well,*" she said, turning from him, "it's true."

"It's not our business, Cora." He didn't see the tremor of her lips.

"So he'll just go on not talking, I suppose! Being afraid of shadows!"

She whirled. "It's *criminal!*" she cried, love and anger bursting from her in a twisted mixture.

"It's got to be done, Cora," he said quietly. "It's our duty."

"*Duty.*" She echoed it with an empty lifelessness in her voice.

She didn't sleep. The liquid flutter of Harry's snoring in her ears, she lay staring at the jump of shadows on the ceiling, a scene enacted in her mind.

A summer's afternoon; the back doorbell ringing. Men standing on the porch, John Carpenter among them, a blanket-covered stillness weighing down his arms, a blank look on his face. In the silence, a drip of water on the sun-baked boards—slowly, unsteadily, like the beats of a dying heart. *He was swimming in the lake, Miz Wheeler and—*

She shuddered on the bed as she had shuddered then—numbly, mutely. The hands beside her were a crumpled whiteness, twisted by remembered anguish. All these years waiting, waiting for a child to bring life into her house again.

At breakfast she was hollow-eyed and drawn. She moved about the kitchen with a willful tread, sliding eggs and pancakes on her husband's plate, pouring coffee, never speaking once.

Then he had kissed her goodbye and she was standing at the living room window watching him trudge down the path to the car. Long after he'd gone, staring at the three envelopes he'd stuck into the side clip of the mailbox.

When Paal came downstairs he smiled at her. She kissed his cheek, then stood behind him, wordless and watching, while he drank his orange juice. The way he sat, the way he held his glass; it was so like—

While Paal ate his cereal she went out to the mailbox and got the three letters, replacing them with three of her own—just in case her husband ever asked the mailman if he'd picked up three letters at their house that morning.

While Paal was eating his eggs, she went down into the cellar and threw the letters into the furnace. The one to Switzerland burned, then the ones to Germany and Sweden. She stirred them with a poker until the pieces broke and disappeared like black confetti in the flames.

Weeks passed; and, with every day, the service of his mind grew weaker.

"Paal, dear, don't you understand?" The patient, loving voice of the woman he needed but feared. "Won't you say it once for me? Just for me? *Paal?*"

He knew there was only love in her but sound would destroy him. It would chain his thoughts—like putting shackles on the wind.

"Would you like to go to school, Paal? Would you? *School?*"

Her face a mask of worried devotion.

"Try to talk, Paal. Just *try.*"

He fought it off with mounting fear. Silence would bring him scraps of meaning from her mind. Then sound returned and grossed each meaning with unwieldy flesh. Meanings joined with sounds. The links formed quickly, frighteningly. He struggled against them. Sounds could cover fragile, darting symbols with a hideous, restraining dough, dough that would be baked in ovens of articulation, then chopped into the stunted lengths of words.

Afraid of the woman, yet wanting to be near the warmth of her, protected by her arms. Like a pendulum he swung from dread to need and back to dread again.

And still the sounds kept shearing at his mind.

We can't wait any longer to hear from them," Harry said. "He'll have to go to school, that's all."

"No," she said.

He put down his newspaper and looked across the living room at her. She kept her eyes on the movements of her knitting needles.

"What do you mean, no?" he asked, irritably. "Every time I mention school you say no. Why *shouldn't* he go to school?"

The needles stopped and were lowered to her lap. Cora stared at them.

"I don't know," she said, "it's just that—" A sigh emptied from her. "I don't know," she said.

"He'll start on Monday," Harry said.

"But he's frightened," she said.

"Sure he's frightened. You'd be frightened too if you couldn't talk and everybody around you was talking. He needs education, that's all."

"But he's not *ignorant,* Harry. I—I swear he understands me sometimes. *Without* talking."

"How?"

"I don't know. But—well, the Nielsens weren't stupid people. They wouldn't just *refuse* to teach him."

"Well, whatever they taught him," Harry said, picking up his paper, "it sure doesn't show."

When they asked Miss Edna Frank over that afternoon to meet the boy she was determined to be impartial.

That Paal Nielsen had been reared in miserable fashion was beyond cavil, but the maiden teacher had decided not to allow the knowledge to affect her attitude. The boy needed understanding. The cruel mistreatment of his parents had to be undone and Miss Frank had elected herself to the office.

Striding with a resolute quickness down German Corners' main artery, she recalled that scene in the Nielsen house when she and Sheriff Wheeler had tried to persuade them to enter Paal in school.

And such a smugness in their faces, thought Miss Frank, remembering. Such a polite disdain. *We do not wish our boy in school,* she heard Professor Nielsen's words again. Just like that, Miss Frank recalled. Arrogant as you please. *We do not wish*—Disgusting attitude.

Well, at least the boy was out of it now. That fire was probably the blessing of his life, she thought.

"We wrote to them four, five weeks ago," the sheriff explained, "and we haven't gotten an answer yet. We can't just let the boy go on the way he is. He needs schooling."

"He most certainly does," agreed Miss Frank, her pale features drawn into their usual sum of unyielding dogmatism. There was a wisp of mustache on her upper lip, her chin came almost to a point. On Halloween the children of German Corners watched the sky above her house.

"He's very shy," Cora said, sensing that harshness in the middle-aged teacher. "He'll be terribly frightened. He'll need a lot of understanding."

"He shall receive it," Miss Frank declared. "But let's see the boy."

Cora led Paal down the steps, speaking to him softly. "Don't be afraid, darling. There's nothing to be afraid of."

Paal entered the room and looked into the eyes of Miss Edna Frank.

Only Cora felt the stiffening of his body—as though, instead of the gaunt virgin, he had looked into the petrifying gaze of the Medusa. Miss Frank and the sheriff did not catch the flare of iris in his bright, green eyes, the minute twitching at one corner of his mouth. None of them could sense the leap of panic in his mind.

Miss Frank sat smiling, holding out her hand.

"Come here, child," she said and, for a moment, the gates slammed shut and hid away the writhing shimmer.

"Come on, darling," Cora said, "Miss Frank is here to help you." She led him forward, feeling beneath her fingers the shuddering of terror in him.

Silence again. And, in the moment of it, Paal felt as though he were walking into a century-sealed tomb. Dead winds gushed out upon him, creatures of frustration slithered on his heart, strange flying jealousies and hates rushed by—all obscured by clouds of twisted memory. It was the purgatory that his father had pictured to him once in telling him of myth and legend. This was no legend though.

Her touch was cool and dry. Dark wrenching terrors ran down her veins and poured into him. Inaudibly, the fragment of a scream tightened his throat. Their eyes met again and Paal saw that, for a second, the woman seemed to know that he was looking at her brain.

Then she spoke and he was free again, limp and staring.

"I think we'll get along just fine," she said.

Maelstrom!

He lurched back on his heels and fell against the sheriff's wife.

All the way across the grounds, it had been growing, growing—as if he were a geiger counter moving towards some fantastic pulsing strata of atomic force. Closer, yet closer, the delicate controls within him stirring, glowing, trembling, reacting with increasing violence to the nearness of power. Even though his sensitivity had been weakened by over three months of sound he felt this now, strongly. As though he walked into a center of vitality.

It was *the young*.

Then the door opened, the voices stopped, and all of it rushed through him like a vast, electric current—all wild and unharnessed. He clung to her, fingers rigid in her skirt, eyes widened, quick breaths falling from his parted lips. His gaze moved shakily across the rows of staring children's faces and waves of distorted energies kept bounding out from them in a snarled, uncontrolled network.

Miss Frank scraped back her chair, stepped down from her six-inch eminence and started down the aisle towards them.

"Good morning," she said, crisply. "We're just about to start our classes for the day."

"I—do hope everything will be all right," Cora said. She glanced down. Paal was looking at the class through a welling haze of tears. "Oh, *Paal*." She leaned over and ran her fingers through his blond hair, a worried look on her face. "Paal, don't be afraid, dear," she whispered.

He looked at her blankly.

"Darling, there's nothing to be—"

"Now just you leave him here," Miss Frank broke in, putting her hand on Paal's shoulder. She ignored the shudder that rippled through him. "He'll be right at home in no time, Mrs. Wheeler. But you've got to leave him by himself."

"Oh, but—" Cora started.

"No, believe me, it's the only way," Miss Frank insisted. "As long as you stay he'll be upset. Believe me. I've seen such things before."

At first he wouldn't let go of Cora but clung to her as the one familiar thing in this whirlpool of frightening newness. It was only when Miss Frank's hard, thin hands held him back that Cora backed off slowly, anxiously, closing the door and cutting off from Paal the sight of her soft pity.

He stood there trembling, incapable of uttering a single word to ask for help. Confused, his mind sent out tenuous shoots of communication but in the undisciplined tangle they were broken off and lost. He drew back quickly and tried, in vain, to cut himself off. All he could manage to do was let the torrent of needling thoughts continue unopposed until they had become a numbing, meaningless surge.

"Now, Paal," he heard Miss Frank's voice and looked up gingerly at her. The hand drew him from the door. "*Come along*."

He didn't understand the words but the brittle sound of them was clear enough, the flow of irrational animosity from her was unmistakable. He stumbled along at her side, threading a thin path of consciousness through the living undergrowth of young, untrained minds; the strange admixture of them with their retention of born sensitivity overlaid with the dulling coat of formal inculcation.

She brought him to the front of the room and stood him there, his chest laboring for breath as if the feelings around him were hands pushing and constraining on his body.

"This is Paal Nielsen, class," Miss Frank announced, and sound drew a momentary blade across the stunted weave of thoughts. "We're going to have to be very patient with him. You see, his mother and father never taught him how to talk."

She looked down at him as a prosecuting lawyer might gaze upon exhibit A.

"He can't understand a word of English," she said.

Silence a moment, writhing. Miss Frank tightened her grip on his shoulder.

"Well, we'll help him learn, won't we, class?"

Faint mutterings arose from them; one thin, piping, "*Yes*, Miss Frank."

"Now, Paal," she said. He didn't turn. She shook his shoulder. "*Paal*," she said.

He looked at her.

"Can you say your name?" she asked. "Paal? Paal Nielsen? Go ahead. Say your name."

Her fingers drew in like talons.

"Say it. Paal. *Pa-al.*"

He sobbed. Miss Frank released her hand.

"You'll learn," she said calmly.

It was not encouragement.

He sat in the middle of it like hooked bait in a current that swirled with devouring mouths, mouths from which endlessly came mind-deadening sounds.

"This is a boat. A boat sails on the water. The men who live on the boat are called sailors."

And, in the primer, the words about the boat printed under a picture of one.

Paal remembered a picture his father had shown him once. It had been a picture of a boat too; but his father had not spoken futile words about the boat. His father had created about the picture every sight and sound heir to it. Great blue rising swells of tide. Gray-green mountain waves, their white tops lashing. Storm winds whistling through the rigging of a bucking, surging, shuddering vessel. The quiet majesty of an ocean sunset, joining, with a scarlet seal, sea and sky.

"This is a farm. Men grow food on the farm. The men who grow food are called farmers."

Words. Empty, with no power to convey the moist, warm feel of earth. The sound of grain fields rustling in the wind like golden seas. The sight of sun setting on a red barn wall. The smell of soft lea winds carrying, from afar, the delicate clank of cowbells.

"This is a forest. A forest is made of trees."

No sense of presence in those black, dogmatic symbols

whether sounded or looked upon. No sound of winds rushing like eternal rivers through the high green canopies. No
smell of pine and birch, oak and maple and hemlock. No
feel of treading on the century-thick carpet of leafy forest
floors.

Words. Blunt, sawed-off lengths of hemmed-in meaning; incapable of evocation, of expansion. Black figures on
white. This is a cat. This is a dog. Cat, dog. This is a man.
This is a woman. Man, woman. Car. Horse. Tree. Desk.
Children. Each word a trap, stalking his mind. A snare set to
enclose fluid and unbounded comprehension.

Every day she stood him on the platform.

"Paal," she would say, pointing at him, "Paal. Say it. Paal."

He couldn't. He stared at her, too intelligent not to
make the connection, to much afraid to seek further.

"Paal." A boney finger prodding at his chest. "Paal. Paal.
Paal."

He fought it. He had to fight it. He blanked his gaze and
saw nothing of the room around him, concentrating only
on his mother's hands. He knew it was a battle. Like a
jelling of sickness, he had felt each new encroachment on
his sensitivity.

"You're not listening, Paal Nielsen!" Miss Frank would
accuse, shaking him. "You're a stubborn, ungrateful boy.
Don't you want to be like *other* children?"

Staring eyes; and her thin, never-to-be-kissed lips stirring, pressing in.

"Sit down," she'd say. He didn't move. She'd move him
off the platform with rigid fingers.

"Sit *down*," she'd say as if talking to a mulish puppy.

Every day.

She was awake in an instant; in another instant, on her feet and hurrying across the darkness of the room. Behind her, Harry slept with laboring breaths. She shut away the sound and let her hand slip off the doorknob as she started across the hall.

"Darling."

He was standing by the window, looking out. As she spoke, he whirled and, in the faint illumination of the night light, she could see the terror written on his face.

"Darling, come to bed." She led him there and tucked him in, then sat beside him, holding his thin, cold hands.

"What is it, dear?"

He looked at her with wide, pained eyes.

"*Oh*—" She bent over and pressed her warm cheek to his. "What are you afraid of?"

In the dark silence it seemed as if a vision of the schoolroom and Miss Frank standing in it crossed her mind.

"Is it the school?" she asked, thinking it only an idea which had occurred to her.

The answer was in his face.

"But school is nothing to be afraid of, darling," she said. "You—"

She saw tears welling in his eyes, and abruptly she drew him up and held him tightly against herself. *Don't be afraid,* she thought. *Darling, please don't be afraid. I'm here and I love you just as much as they did. I love you even more—*

Paal drew back. He stared at her as if he didn't understand.

As the car pulled up in back of the house, Werner saw a woman turn away from the kitchen window.

"If we'd only heard from you," said Wheeler, "but there was never a word. You can't blame us for adopting the boy. We did what we thought was best."

Werner nodded wih short, distracted movements of his head.

"I understand," he said quietly. "We received no letters, however."

They sat in the car in silence, Werner staring through the windshield, Wheeler looking at his hands.

Holger and Fanny *dead,* Werner was thinking. A horrible discovery to make. The boy exposed to the cruel blunderings of people who did not understand. That was, in a way, even more horrible.

Wheeler was thinking of those letters and of Cora. He should have written again. Still, those letters should have reached Europe. Was it possible they were all missent?

"Well," he said, finally, "you'll—want to see the boy."

"Yes," said Werner.

The two men pushed open the car doors and got out. They walked across the backyard and up the wooden porch steps. Have you taught him how to speak?—Werner almost said but couldn't bring himself to ask. The concept of a boy like Paal exposed to the blunt, deadening forces of usual speech was something he felt uncomfortable thinking about.

"I'll get my wife," said Wheeler. "The living room's in there."

After the sheriff had gone up the back stairs, Werner walked slowly through the hall and into the front room. There he took off his raincoat and hat and dropped them over the back of a wooden chair. Upstairs he could hear the faint sound of voices—a man and woman. The woman sounded upset.

When he heard footsteps, he turned from the window.

The sheriff's wife entered beside her husband. She was smiling politely, but Werner knew she wasn't happy to see him there.

"Please sit down," she said.

He waited until she was in a chair, then settled down on the couch.

"What is it you want?" asked Mrs. Wheeler.

"Did your husband tell you—?"

"He told me who you were," she interrupted, "but not why you want to see Paul."

"*Paul?*" asked Werner, surprised.

"We—" Her hands sought out each other nervously. "—we changed it to Paul. It—seemed more appropriate. For a Wheeler, I mean."

"I see." Werner nodded politely.

Silence.

"Well," Werner said then, "you wish to know why I am here to see—the boy. I will explain as briefly as possible.

"Ten years ago, in Heidelberg, four married couples— the Elkenbergs, the Kalders, the Nielsens, and my wife and

I—decided to try an experiment on our children—some not yet born. An experiment of the mind.

"We had accepted, you see, the proposition that ancient man, deprived of the dubious benefit of language, had been telepathic."

Cora started in her chair.

"Further," Werner went on, not noticing, "that the basic organic source of this ability is still functioning though no longer made use of—a sort of ethereal tonsil, a higher appendix—not used but neither useless.

"So we began our work, each searching for physiological facts while, at the same time, developing the ability in our children. Monthly correspondence was exchanged, a systematic methodology of training was arrived at slowly. Eventually, we planned to establish a colony with the grown children, a colony to be gradually consolidated until these abilities would become second nature to its members.

"Paal is one of these children."

Wheeler looked almost dazed.

"This is a *fact*?" he asked.

"A fact," said Werner.

Cora sat numbly in her chair staring at the tall German. She was thinking about the way Paal seemed to understand her without words. Thinking of his fear of the school and Miss Frank. Thinking of how many times she had woken up and gone to him even though he didn't make a sound.

"What?" she asked, looking up as Werner spoke.

"I say—may I see the boy now?"

"He's in school," she said. "He'll be home in—"

She stopped as a look of almost revulsion crossed Werner's face.

"*School?*" he asked.

Paal Nielsen, stand."

The young boy slid from his seat and stood beside the desk. Miss Frank gestured to him once and, more like an old man than a boy, he trudged up to the platform and stood beside her as he always did.

"Straighten up," Miss Frank demanded. "Shoulders back."

The shoulders moved, the back grew flat.

"What's your name?" asked Miss Frank.

The boy pressed his lips together slightly. His swallowing made a dry, rattling noise.

"*What is your name?*"

Silence in the classroom except for the restive stirring of the young. Erratic currents of their thought deflected off him like random winds.

"*Your name,*" she said.

He made no reply.

The virgin teacher looked at him and, in the moment that she did, through her mind ran memories of her childhood. Of her gaunt, mania-driven mother keeping her for hours at a time in the darkened front parlor, sitting at the great round table, her fingers arched over the smoothly worn ouija board—making her try to communicate with her dead father.

Memories of those terrible years were still with her—always with her. Her minor sensitivity being abused and twisted into knots until she hated every single thing about perception. Perception was an evil, full of suffering and anguish.

The boy must be freed of it.

"Class," she said, "I want you all to think of Paal's name." (This was his name no matter what Mrs. Wheeler chose to call him.) "Just think of it. Don't say it. Just think: Paal, Paal, Paal. When I count three. Do you understand?"

They stared at her, some nodding. "*Yes*, Miss Frank," piped up her only faithful.

"All right," she said, "One—two—*three*."

It flung into his mind like the blast of a hurricane, pounding and tearing at his hold on wordless sensitivity. He trembled on the platform, his mouth fallen ajar.

The blast grew stronger, all the power of the young directed into a single, irresistible force. Paal, *Paal, PAAL!!* It screamed into the tissues of his brain.

Until, at the very peak of it, when he thought his head would explode, it was all cut away by the voice of Miss Frank scalpelling into his mind.

"Say it! Paal!"

Here he comes," said Cora. She turned from the window. "Before he gets here, I want to apologize for my rudeness."

"Not at all," said Werner, distractedly, "I understand perfectly. Naturally, you would think that I had come to take the boy away. As I have said, however, I have no legal powers over him—being no relation. I simply want to see him as the child of my two colleagues—whose shocking death I have only now learned of."

He saw the woman's throat move and picked out the leap of guilty panic in her mind. She had destroyed the letters her husband wrote. Werner knew it instantly but said nothing. He sensed that the husband also knew it; she would have enough trouble as it was.

They heard Paal's footsteps on the bottom step of the front porch.

"I *will* take him out of school," Cora said.

"Perhaps not," said Werner, looking towards the door. In spite of everything he felt his heartbeat quicken, felt the fingers of his left hand twitch in his lap. Without a word, he sent out the message. It was a greeting the four couples had decided on; a sort of password.

Telepathy, he thought, *is the communication of impressions of any kind from one mind to another independently of the recognized channels of sense.*

Werner sent it twice before the front door opened.

Paal stood there, motionless.

Werner saw recognition in his eyes, but, in the boy's mind, was only confused uncertainty. The misted vision of Werner's face crossed it. In his mind, all the people had existed—Werner, Elkenberg, Kalder, all their children. But now it was locked up and hard to capture. The face disappeared.

"Paul, this is Mister Werner," Cora said.

Werner did not speak. He sent the message out again— with such force that Paal could not possibly miss it. He saw a look of uncomprehending dismay creep across the boy's features, as if Paal suspected that something was happening yet could not imagine what.

The boy's face grew more confused. Cora's eyes moved concernedly from him to Werner and back again. Why didn't Werner speak? She started to say something, then remembered what the German had said.

"Say, what—?" Wheeler began until Cora waved her hand and stopped him.

Paal, think!—Werner thought desperately—*Where is your mind?*

Suddenly, there was a great, wracking sob in the boy's throat and chest. Werner shuddered.

"My name is Paal," the boy said.

The voice made Werner's flesh crawl. It was unfinished, like a puppet voice, thin, wavering, and brittle.

"My name is Paal."

He couldn't stop saying it. It was as if he were whipping himself on, knowing what had happened and trying to suffer as much as possible with the knowledge.

"My name is Paal. My name is Paal." An endless, frightening babble; in it, a panic-stricken boy seeking out an unknown power which had been torn from him.

"My name is Paal." Even held tightly in Cora's arms, he said it. "My name is Paal." Angrily, pitiably, endlessly. "*My name is Paal. My name is Paal.*"

Werner closed his eyes.

Lost.

Wheeler offered to take him back to the bus station, but Werner told him he'd rather walk. He said good-bye to the sheriff and asked him to relay his regrets to Mrs. Wheeler, who had taken the sobbing boy up to his room.

Now, in the beginning fall of a fine, mistlike rain, Werner walked away from the house, from Paal.

It was not something easily judged, he was thinking. There was no right and wrong of it. Definitely, it was not a case of evil versus good. Mrs. Wheeler, the sheriff, the boy's teacher, the people of German Corners—they had, probably, all meant well. Understandably, they had been outraged at the idea of a seven-year-old boy not having been taught to speak by his parents. Their actions were, in light of that, justifiable and good.

It was simply that, so often, evil could come of misguided good.

No, it was better left as it was. To take Paal back to Europe—back to the others—would be a mistake. He could if he wanted to; all the couples had exchanged papers giving each other the right to take over rearing of the children should anything happen to the parents. But it would only confuse Paal further. He had been a trained sensitive, not a born one. Although, by the principle they all worked on, all children were born with the atavistic ability to telepath, it was so easy to lose, so difficult to recapture.

Werner shook his head. It was a pity. The boy was without his parents, without his talent, even without his name.

He had lost everything.

Well, perhaps, not everything.

As he walked, Werner sent his mind back to the house to discover them standing at the window of Paal's room, watching sunset cast its fiery light on German Corners. Paal was clinging to the sheriff's wife, his cheek pressed to her side. The final terror of losing his awareness had not faded but there was something else counterbalancing it. Something Cora Wheeler sensed yet did not fully realize.

Paal's parents had not loved him. Werner knew this. Caught up in the fascination of their work they had not had the time to love him as a child. Kind, yes, affectionate, always; still, they had regarded Paal as their experiment in flesh.

Which was why Cora Wheeler's love was, in part, as strange a thing to Paal as all the crushing horrors of speech. It would not remain so. For, in that moment when the last of his gift had fled, leaving his mind a naked rawness, she had been there with her love, to soothe away the pain. And always would be there.

"Did you find who you were looking for?" the gray-haired woman at the counter asked Werner as she served him coffee.

"Yes. Thank you," he said.

"Where was he?" asked the woman.

Werner smiled.

"At home," he said.

THE CREEPING TERROR

THESIS SUBMITTED AS PARTIAL
REQUIREMENT FOR MASTER OF ARTS DEGREE

The phenomenon known in scientific circles as the Los Angeles Movement came to light in the year 1982 when Doctor Albert Grimsby, A.B., B.S., A.M., Ph.D., professor of physics at the California Institute of Technology, made an unusual discovery.

I have made an unusual discovery," said Doctor Grimsby.

"What is that?" asked Doctor Maxwell.

"Los Angeles is alive."

Doctor Maxwell blinked.

"I beg your pardon," he said.

"I can understand your incredulity," said Doctor Grimsby. "Nevertheless . . ."

He drew Doctor Maxwell to the laboratory bench.

"Look into this microscope," he said, "under which I have isolated a piece of Los Angeles."

Doctor Maxwell looked. He raised his head, a look of aston-
ishment on his face.

"It moves," he said.

Having made this strange discovery, Doctor Grimsby, oddly enough, saw fit to promulgate it only in the smallest degree. It appeared as a one-paragraph item in the *Science News Letter* of June 2, 1982, under the heading: CALTECH PHYSICIST FINDS SIGNS OF LIFE IN L.A.

Perhaps due to unfortunate phrasing, perhaps to normal lack of interest, the item aroused neither attention nor comment. This unfortunate negligence proved ever after a plague to the man originally responsible for it. In later years it became known as "Grimsby's Blunder."

Thus was introduced to a then unresponsive nation a phenomenon which was to become in the following years a most shocking threat to that nation's very existence.

Of late, researchers have discovered that knowledge concerning the Los Angeles Movement predates Doctor Grimsby's find by years. Indeed, hints of this frightening crisis are to be found in works published as much as fifteen years prior to the ill-fated "Caltech Disclosure."

Concerning Los Angeles, the distinguished journalist, John Gunther, wrote: "What distinguishes it is . . . its octopus-like growth."[1]

---

1 John Gunther, *Inside U.S.A.*, p. 44.

Yet another reference to Los Angeles mentions that: "In its amoeba-like growth it has spread in all directions. . . ."[2]

Thus can be seen primitive approaches to the phenomenon which are as perceptive as they are unaware. Although there is no present evidence to indicate that any person during that early period actually knew of the fantastic process, there can hardly be any doubt that many *sensed* it, if only imperfectly.

Active speculation regarding freakish nature behavior began in July and August of 1982. During a period of approximately forty-seven days the states of Arizona and Utah in their entirety and great portions of New Mexico and lower Colorado were inundated by rains that frequently bettered the ten-inch mark.

Such water fall in previously arid sections aroused great agitation and discussion. First theories placed responsibility for this uncommon rainfall on previous southwestern atomic tests.[3] Government disclaiming of this possibility seemed to increase rather than eliminate mass credulity to this later disproved supposition.

Other "precipitation postulations" as they were then known in investigative parlance can be safely relegated to the category of "crackpotia."[4] These include theories that

2 Henry G. Alsberg (ed.), *The American Guide,* p. 1200.

3 Symmes Chadwick, "Will We Drown the World?" *Southwestern Review IV* (Summer 1982), p. 698 ff.

4 Guillaume Gaulte, "Les Théories de l'Eau de Ciel Sont Cuckoo," *Jaune Journale* (August 1982).

excess commercial airflights were upsetting the natural balance of the clouds, that deranged Indian rainmakers had
unwittingly come upon some lethal condensation factor and
were applying it beyond all sanity, that strange frost from
outer space was seeding Earth's overhead and causing this
inordinate precipitation.

And, as seems an inevitable concomitant to all alien de-
portment in nature, hypotheses were propounded that this
heavy rainfall presaged *Deluge II.* It is clearly recorded that
several minor religious groups began hasty construction of
"Salvation Arks." One of these arks can still be seen on the
outskirts of the small town of Dry Rot, New Mexico, built
on a small hill, "still waiting for the flood."[5]

Then came that memorable day when the name of
farmer Cyrus Mills became a household word.

*T*arnation!" *said farmer Mills.*

*He gaped in rustic amazement at the object he had come across
in his corn field. He approached it cautiously. He prodded it with a
sausage finger.*

"Tarnation," he repeated, less volubly.

Jason Gullwhistle of the United States Experimental Farm
Station No. 3, *Nebraska, drove his station wagon out to farmer
Mills's farm in answer to an urgent phone call. Farmer Mills took
Mr. Gullwhistle out to the object.*

*"That's odd," said Jason Gullwhistle. "It looks like an orange
tree."*

---

5 Harry L. Schuler, "Not Long for This World," *South Orange Literary Review,* XL (Sept. 1982), p. 214.

Close investigation revealed the truth of this remark. It was, in-deed, an orange tree.

"Incredible," said Jason Gullwhistle. "An orange tree in the middle of a Nebraska corn field. I never."

Later they returned to the house for a lemonade and there found Mrs. Mills in halter and shorts wearing sunglasses and an old chewed-up fur jacket she had exhumed from her crumbling hope chest.

"Think I'll drive into Hollywood," said Mrs. Mills, sixty-five if she was a day.

By nightfall every wire service had embraced the item, every paper of any prominence whatever had featured it as a humorous insert on page one.

Within a week, however, the humor had vanished as reports came pouring in from every corner of the state of Nebraska as well as portions of Iowa, Kansas and Colorado; reports of citrus trees discovered in corn and wheat fields as well as more alarming reports relative to eccentric behavior in the rural populace.

Addiction to the wearing of scanty apparel became noticeable, an inexplicable rise in the sales of frozen orange juice manifested itself and oddly similar letters were received by dozens of chambers of commerce; letters which heatedly demanded the immediate construction of condominiums, supermarkets, tennis courts, drive-in theaters and drive-in restaurants and which complained of smog.

But it was not until a marked decrease in daily temperatures and an equally marked increase of unfathomable citrus tree growth began to imperil the corn and wheat crop that serious action was taken. Local farm groups organized spraying operations but to little or no avail. Orange, lemon and grapefruit trees continued to flourish in geometric proliferation and a nation, at long last, became alarmed.

A seminar of the country's top scientists met in Ragweed, Nebraska, the geographical center of this multiplying plague, to discuss possibilities.

*D*ynamic tremors in the alluvial substrata," said Doctor Kenneth Loam of the University of Denver.

"Mass chemical disorder in soil composition," said Spencer Smith of the Dupont Laboratories.

"Momentous gene mutation in the corn seed," said Professor Jeremy Brass of Kansas College.

"Violent contraction of the atmospheric dome," said Professor Lawson Hinkson of MIT.

"Displacement of orbit," said Roger Cosmos of the Hayden Planetarium.

"I'm scared," said a little man from Purdue.

What positive results emerged from this body of speculative genius is yet to be appraised. History records that a closer labeling of the cause of this unusual behavior in Nature and Man occurred in early October of 1982 when Associate Professor David Silver, young research physicist at the University of Missouri, published in *The Scientific American* an article entitled, "The Collecting of Evidences."

In this brilliant essay, Professor Silver first voiced the opinion that all the apparently disconnected occurrences were, in actuality, superficial revelations of one underlying phenomenon. To the moment of this article, scant attention had been paid to the erratic behavior of people in the affected areas. Professor Silver attributed this behavior to the same cause which had effected the alien growth of citrus trees.

The final deductive link was forged, oddly enough, in a Sunday supplement of the now defunct Hearst newspaper syndicate.[6] The author of this piece, a professional article writer, in doing research for an article, stumbled across the paragraph recounting Doctor Grimsby's discovery. Seeing in this a most salable feature, he wrote an article combining the theses of Doctor Grimsby and Professor Silver and emerging with his own amateur concept which, strange to say, was absolutely correct. (This fact was later obscured in the severe litigation that arose when Professors Grimsby and Silver brought suit against the author for not consulting them before writing the article.)

Thus did it finally become known that Los Angeles, like some gigantic fungus, was overgrowing the land.

A period of gestation followed during which various publications in the country slowly built up the import of the Los Angeles Movement, until it became a national by-word. It was during this period that a fertile-minded columnist dubbed Los Angeles "Ellie, the Meandering Metropolis,"[7] a title later reduced merely to "Ellie"—a term which became as common to the American mind as "ham and eggs" or "World War II."

---

6 H. Braham, "Is Los Angeles Alive?" *Los Angeles Sunday Examiner*, 29 Oct. 1982.

7 "Ellieitis: Its Symptoms," AMA pamphlet (fall 1982).

Now began a cycle of data collection and an attempt by various of the prominent sciences to analyze the Los Angeles Movement with a regard to arresting its strange pilgrimage which had now spread into parts of South Dakota, Missouri, Arkansas and as far as the sovereign state of Texas. (To the mass convulsion this caused in the Lone Star State a separate paper might be devoted.)

REPUBLICANS DEMAND FULL INVESTIGATION
Claim L.A. Movement Subversive Camouflage

After a hasty dispatch of agents to all points in the infected area, the American Medical Association promulgated throughout the nation a list of symptoms by which all inhabitants might be forewarned of the approaching terror.

SYMPTOMS OF "ELLIEITIS"[7]

1. An unnatural craving for any of the citrus fruits whether in solid or liquid form.

2. Partial or complete loss of geographical distinction. (i.e., A person in Kansas City might speak of driving down to San Diego for the weekend.)

3. An unnatural desire to possess a motor vehicle.

4. An unnatural appetite for motion pictures and motion picture previews. (Including a subsidiary symptom, not all-inclusive but nevertheless a distinct menace. This

is the insatiable hunger of young girls to
become movie stars.)

5. A taste for weird apparel. (Including fur
jackets, shorts, halters, slacks, sandals,
blue jeans and bathing suits—all usually
of excessive color.)

This list, unfortunately, proved most inadequate for its
avowed purpose. It did not mention, for one thing, the ad-
verse effect of excess sunlight on residents of the northern
states. With the expected approach to winter being fore-
stalled stalled indefinitely, numerous unfortunates, unable to
adjust to this alteration, became neurotic and, often, lost
their senses completely.

The story of Matchbox, North Dakota, a small town in
the northernmost part of that state, is typical of accounts
which flourished throughout the late fall and winter of 1982.

The citizens of this ill-fated town went berserk to a man
waiting for the snow and, eventually running amuck, burned
their village to the ground.

The pamphlet also failed to mention the psychological
phenomenon known later as "Beach Seeking,"[8] a delusion
under which masses of people, wearing bathing suits and
carrying towels and blankets, wandered helplessly across the
plains and prairies searching for the Pacific Ocean.

In October, the Los Angeles Movement (the process was
given this more staid title in late September by Professor

---

8 Fritz Felix DerKatt, "Das Beachen Seeken," *Einzweidrei* (Nov. 1982).

Augustus Wrench in a paper sent to the National Council of American Scientists) picked up momentum and, in a space of ten days, had engulfed Arkansas, Missouri and Minnesota and) was creeping rapidly into the borderlands of Illinois, Wisconsin, Tennessee, Mississippi and Louisiana. Smog drifted across the nation.

Up to this point, citizens on the east coast had been interested in the phenomenon but not overly perturbed since distance from the diseased territory had lent detachment. Now, however, as the Los Angeles city limits stalked closer and closer to them, the coastal region became alarmed.

Legislative activity in Washington was virtually terminated as Congressmen were inundated with letters of protest and demand. A special committee, heretofore burdened by general public apathy in the east, now became enlarged by the added membership of several distinguished Congressmen, and a costly probe into the problem ensued.

It was this committee that, during the course of its televised hearings, unearthed a secret group known as the L.A. Firsters.

This insidious organization seemed to have sprung almost spontaneously from the general chaos of the Los Angeles envelopment. General credence was given for a short time that it was another symptom of "Ellieitis." Intense interrogation, however, revealed the existence of L.A. Firster cells in East Coast cities that could not possibly have been subject to the dread virus at that point.

This revelation struck terror into the heart of a nation. The presence of such calculated subversion in this moment of trial almost unnerved the national will. For it was not merely an organization loosely joined by emotional binds. This faction possessed a carefully wrought hierarchy of men and women which was plotting the overthrow of the national government. Nationwide distribution of literature had begun almost with the advent of the Los Angeles Movement. This literature, with the cunning of insurgent casuistry, painted a roseate picture of the future of—The United States of Los Angeles!

PEOPLE ARISE![9]

People arise! Cast off the shackles
of reaction! What sense is there in
opposing the march of PROGRESS! It
is inevitable!—and you the people
of this glorious land—a land
bought dearly with *your* blood and
your tears —should realize that *Nature herself* supports the L.A. FIRSTERS!
How?—you ask. How does Nature
support this glorious adventure? The
question is simple enough to answer.
NATURE HAS SUPPORTED THE L.A.
FIRSTER MOVEMENT FOR THE BETTER-
MENT OF YOU! AND *YOU*!
Here are a few facts:
In those states that have been
blessed
    1. Rheumatism has dropped 52%;

---

9 *The Los Angeles Manifesto*, L.A. Firster Press (Winter 1982).

2. Pneumonia has dropped 61%;

3. Frostbite has *vanished;*

4. Incidence of the COMMON COLD has dropped 73%!

Is this bad news? Are these the changes brought about by anti-PROGRESS?

NO!!!

Wherever Los Angeles has gone, the deserts have fled, adding millions of new fertile acres to our beloved land. Where once there was only sand and cactus and *bleached bones*, are now plants and trees and FLOWERS!

This pamphlet closes with a couplet which aroused a nation to fury:

> *Sing out O land, with flag unfurled!*
> *Los Angeles! Tomorrow's World!*

The exposure of the L.A. Firsters caused a tide of reaction to sweep the country. Rage became the keynote of this counterrevolution; rage at the subtlety with which the L.A. Firsters had distorted truth in their literature; rage at their arrogant assumption that the country would inevitably fall to Los Angeles.

Slogans of "Down with the L.A. Lovers!" and "Send Them Back Where They Came From!" rang throughout

the land. A measure was forced through Congress and pres-
idential signature outlawing the group and making membership in it the offense of treason. Rabid groups attached a
rider to this measure which would have enforced the out-
lawry, seizure and destruction of all tennis and beach supply
manufacturing. Here, however, the N.A.M. stepped into the
scene and, through the judicious use of various pressure
means, defeated the attempt.

Despite this quick retaliation, the L.A. Firsters continued underground and at least one fatality of its persistent
agitation was the state of Missouri.

In some manner, as yet undisclosed, the L.A. Firsters
gained control of the state legislature and jockeyed through an
amendment to the constitution of Missouri which was hastily
ratified and made the Show-Me State the first area in the
country to legally make itself a part of Los Angeles County.

UTTER MCKINLEY OPENS

FIVE NEW PARLORS

IN THE SOUTHWEST

In the succeeding months there emerged a notable upsurge
in the production of automobiles, particularly those of the
convertible variety. In those states affected by the Los Angeles Movement, every citizen, apparently, had acquired that
symptom of "Ellieitis" known as *automania*. The car industry entered accordingly upon a period of peak production,
its factories turning out automobiles twenty-four hours a
day, seven days a week.

In conjunction with this increase in automotive fabrication, there began a near maniacal splurge in the building of drive-in restaurants and theaters. These sprang up with mushroomlike celerity through Western and Midwestern United States, their planning going beyond all feasibility. Typical of these thoughtless projects was the endeavor to hollow out a mountain and convert it into a drive-in theater.[10]

As the month of December approached, the Los Angeles Movement engulfed Illinois, Wisconsin, Mississippi, half of Tennessee and was lapping at the shores of Indiana, Kentucky and Alabama. (No mention will be made of the profound effect this movement had on racial segregation in the South, this subject demanding a complete investigation in itself.)

It was about this time that a wave of religious passion obsessed the nation. As is the nature of the human mind suffering catastrophe, millions turned to religion. Various cults had in this calamity grist for their metaphysical mills.

Typical of these were the San Bernardino Vine Worshipers who claimed Los Angeles to be the reincarnation of their deity Ochsalia—The Vine Divine. The San Diego Sons of the Weed claimed in turn that Los Angeles was a sister embodiment of their deity which they claimed had been creeping for three decades prior to the Los Angeles Movement.

Unfortunately for all concerned, a small fascistic clique began to usurp control of many of these otherwise harmless cults, emphasizing dominance through "power and energy."

10 L. Savage, "A Report on the Grand Teton Drive-In," *Fortune* (Jan. 1983).

As a result, these religious bodies too often degenerated into mere fronts for political cells which plotted the overthrow of the government for purposes of self-aggrandizement. (Secret documents discovered in later years revealed the intention of one perfidious brotherhood of converting the Pentagon Building into an indoor race track.)

During a period beginning in September and extending for years, there also ensued a studied expansion of the motion-picture industry. Various of the major producers opened branch studios throughout the country (for example, MGM built one in Terre Haute, Paramount in Cincinnati and Twentieth-Century Fox in Tulsa). The Screen Writer's Guild initiated branch offices in every large city and the term "Hollywood" became even more of a misnomer than it had previously been.

Motion picture output more than quadrupled as theaters of all description were hastily erected everywhere west of the Mississippi, sometimes wall to wall for blocks.[11] These buildings were rarely well constructed and often collapsed within weeks of their "grand openings."

Yet, in spite of the incredible number of theaters, motion pictures exceeded them in quantity (if not quality). It was in compensation for this economically dangerous situation that the studios inaugurated the expedient practice of burning films in order to maintain the stability of the price floor. This aroused great antipathy among the smaller studios who did not produce enough films to burn any.

---

11 "Gulls Creek Gets Its Forty-Eighth Theater." *The Arkansas Post-Journal,* 12 March 1983.

Another liability involved in the production of motion pictures was the geometric increase in difficulties raised by small but voluble pressure groups.

One typical coterie was the Anti-Horse League of Dallas which put up strenuous opposition to the utilization of horses in films. This, plus the increasing incidence of car owning which had made horse breeding unprofitable, made the production of Western films (as they had been known) an impossible chore. Thus was it that the so-called "Western" gravitated rapidly toward the "drawing room" drama.

SECTION OF A TYPICAL SCREENPLAY[12]

Tex D'Urberville comes riding into Doomtown on the Colorado, his Jaguar raising a cloud of dust in the sleepy western town. He parks in front of the Golden Sovereign Saloon and steps out. He is a tall, rangy cowhand, impeccably attired in waistcoat and fawn-skin trousers with a ten-gallon hat, boots and pearl-gray spats. A heavy sixgun is belted at his waist. He carries a gold-topped malacca cane.

He enters the saloon and every man there scatters from the room, leaving only Tex and a scowling hulk of a man at the other end of the bar. This is Dirty Ned Updyke, local ruffian and gunman.

TEX *(Removing his white gloves and, pretending*

12 Maxwell Brande, "Altercation at Deadwood Spa," Epigram Studios (April 1983).

he does not see Dirty Ned, addressing the
bartender): Pour me a whiskey and seltzer
will you, Roger, there's a good fellow.
ROGER: *Yes sir.*
Dirty Ned scowls over his apéritif but does not
dare to reach for his Webley Automatic pistol
which is concealed in a holster beneath his tweed
jacket.

   Now Tex D'Urberville allows his icy blue
eyes to move slowly about the room until they rest
on the craven features of Dirty Ned.
TEX: *So . . . you're the beastly cad what shot my*
   brother.
Instantly they draw their cane swords and, ap-
proaching, salute each other grimly.

An additional result not to be overlooked was the effect of
increased film production on politics. The need for high-
salaried workers such as writers, actors, directors and plumbers
was intense and this mass of *nouveau riche,* having come
upon good times so relatively abruptly, acquired a definite
guilt neurosis which resulted in their intensive participation
in the so-called "liberal" and "progressive" groups. This
swelling of radical activity did much to alter the course of
American political history. (This subject being another
which requires separate inquiry for a proper evaluation of
its many and varied ramifications.)

Two other factors of this period which may be mentioned
briefly are the increase in divorce due to the relaxation of

divorce laws in every state affected by the Los Angeles Movement and the slow but eventually complete bans placed upon tennis and beach supplies by a rabid but powerful group within the N.A.M. This ban led inexorably to a brief span of time which paralleled the so-called "Prohibition" period the the 1920s. During this infamous period, thrill seekers attended the many bootleg tennis courts throughout the country, which sprang up wherever perverse public demand made them profitable ventures for unscrupulous men.

In the first days of January of 1983 the Los Angeles Movement reached almost to the Atlantic shoreline. Panic spread through New England and the southern coastal region. The country and, ultimately, Washington reverberated with cries of "*Stop Los Angeles!*" and all processes of government ground to a virtual halt in the ensuing chaos. Law enforcement atrophied, crime waves spilled across the nation and conditions became so grave that even the outlawed L.A. Firsters held revival meetings in the street.

On February 11, 1983, the Los Angeles Movement forded the Hudson River and invaded Manhattan Island. Flame-throwing tanks proved futile against the invincible flux. Within a week the subways were closed and car purchases had trebled.

By March 1983 the only unaltered states in the union were Maine, Vermont, New Hampshire and Massachusetts. This was later explained by the lethargic adaptation of the fungi

to the rocky New England soil and to the immediate in-
clement weather.

These northern states, cornered and helpless, resorted to
extraordinary measures in a hopeless bid to ward off the awful incrustation. Several of them legalized the mercy killing
of any person discovered to have acquired the taint of
"Ellieitis." Newspaper reports of shootings, stabbings, poi-
sonings and strangulations became so common in those days
of "The Last-Ditch Defense" that newspapers inaugurated a
daily section of their contents to such reports.

*Boston, Mass. April 13, AP—Last rites were held today for Mr.
Abner Scrounge who was shot after being found in his garage at-
tempting to remove the top of his Rolls Royce with a can opener.*

The history of the gallant battle of Boston to retain its es-
sential dignity would, alone, make up a large work. The
story of how the intrepid citizens of this venerable city refused to surrender their rights, choosing mass suicide rather
than submission is a tale of enduring courage and majestic
struggle against insurmountable odds.

What happened after the movement was contained
within the boundaries of the United States (a name soon
discarded) is data for another paper. A brief mention, however, may be made of the immense social endeavor which
became known as the "Bacon and Waffles" movement,
which sought to guarantee $750 per month for every per-
son in Los Angeles over forty years of age.

With this incentive before the people, state legislatures
were helpless before an avalanche of public demand and,

within three years, the entire nation was a part of Los Angeles. The government seat was in Beverly Hills and ambassadors had been hastened to all foreign countries within a short period of time.

Ten years later the North American continent fell and Los Angeles was creeping rapidly down the Isthmus of Panama.

Then came that ill-fated day in 1994.

On the island of Pingo Pongo, Maona, daughter of Chief Luana, approached her father.

"Omu la golu si mongo," she said.

(Anyone for tennis?)

Whereupon her father, having read the papers, speared her on the spot and ran screaming from the hut.

SHOCK WAVE

I tell you there's something wrong with her," said Mr. Moffat. Cousin Wendall reached for the sugar bowl.

"Then they're right," he said. He spooned the sugar into his coffee.

"They are *not,*" said Mr. Moffat, sharply. "They most certainly are *not.*"

"If she isn't working," Wendall said.

"She *was* working until just a month or so ago," said Mr. Moffat. "She was working *fine* when they decided to replace her the first of the year."

His fingers, pale and yellowed, lay tensely on the table. His eggs and coffee were untouched and cold before him.

"Why are you so upset?" asked Wendall. "She's just an organ."

"*She is more,*" Mr. Moffat said. "She was in before the church was even finished. Eighty years she's been there. *Eighty.*"

"That's pretty long," said Wendall, crunching jelly-smeared toast. "Maybe too long."

"There's nothing wrong with her," defended Mr. Moffat.

"Leastwise, there never was before. That's why I want you to sit in the loft with me this morning."

"How come you haven't had an organ man look at her?" Wendall asked.

"He'd just agree with the rest of them," said Mr. Moffat, sourly. "He'd just say she's too old, too worn."

"Maybe she is," said Wendall.

"*She is not.*" Mr. Moffat trembled fitfully.

"Well, I don't know," said Wendall, "she's pretty old though."

"She worked fine before," said Mr. Moffat. He stared into the blackness of his coffee. "The gall of them," he muttered. "Planning to get rid of her. The *gall.*"

He closed his eyes.

"Maybe she knows," he said.

The clock-like tapping of their heels perforated the stillness in the lobby.

"This way," Mr. Moffat said.

Wendall pushed open the arm-thick door and the two men spiraled up the marble staircase. On the second floor, Mr. Moffat shifted the briefcase to his other hand and searched his keyring. He unlocked the door and they entered the musty darkness of the loft. They moved through the silence, two faint, echoing sounds.

"Over here," said Mr. Moffat.

"Yes, I see," said Wendall.

The old man sank down on the glass-smooth bench and turned the small lamp on. A wedge of bulb light forced aside the shadows.

"Think the sun'll show?" asked Wendall.

"Don't know," said Mr. Moffat.

He unlocked and rattled up the organ's rib-skinned top, then raised the music rack. He pushed the finger-worn switch across its slot.

In the brick room to their right there was a sudden hum, a mounting rush of energy. The air-gauge needle quivered across its dial.

"She's alive now," Mr. Moffat said.

Wendall grunted in amusement and walked across the loft. The old man followed.

"What do you think?" he asked inside the brick room.

Wendall shrugged.

"Can't tell," he said. He looked at the turning of the motor. "Single-phase induction," he said. "Runs by magnetism."

He listened. "Sounds all right to me," he said.

He walked across the small room.

"What's this?" he asked, pointing.

"Relay machines," said Mr. Moffat. "Keep the channels filled with wind."

"And this is the fan?" asked Wendall.

The old man nodded.

"Mmm-hmm." Wendall turned. "Looks all right to me," he said.

They stood outside looking up at the pipes. Above the glossy wood of the enclosure box, they stood like giant pencils painted gold.

"Big," said Wendall.

"She's *beautiful*," said Mr. Moffat.

"Let's hear her," Wendall said.

They walked back to the keyboards and Mr. Moffat sat before them. He pulled out a stop and pressed a key into its bed.

A single tone poured out into the shadowed air. The old man pressed a volume pedal and the note grew louder. It pierced the air, tone and overtones bouncing off the church dome like diamonds hurled from a sling.

Suddenly, the old man raised his hand.

"*Did you hear?*" he asked.

"Hear what?"

"It *trembled*," Mr. Moffat said.

As people entered the church, Mr. Moffat was playing Bach's chorale prelude *Aus der Tiefe rufe ich (From the Depths, I Cry)*. His fingers moved certainly on the manual keys, his spindling shoes walked a dance across the pedals; and the air was rich with moving sound.

Wendall leaned over to whisper, "There's the sun."

Above the old man's gray-wreathed pate, the sunlight came filtering through the stained-glass window. It passed across the rack of pipes with a mistlike radiance.

Wendall leaned over again.

"Sounds all right to me," he said.

"*Wait,*" said Mr. Moffat.

Wendall grunted. Stepping to the loft edge, he looked down at the nave. The three-aisled flow of people was branching off into rows. The echoing of their movements scaled up like insect scratchings. Wendall watched them as they settled in the brown-wood pews. Above and all about them moved the organ's music.

"Sssst."

Wendall turned and moved back to his cousin.

"What is it?" he asked.

"Listen."

Wendall cocked his head.

"Can't hear anything but the organ and the motor," he said.

"That's *it*," the old man whispered. *"You're not supposed to hear the motor."*

Wendall shrugged. "So?" he said.

The old man wet his lips. "I think it's starting," he murmured.

Below, the lobby doors were being shut. Mr. Moffat's gaze fluttered to his watch propped against the music rack, thence to the pulpit where the Reverend had appeared. He made of the chorale prelude's final chord a shimmering pyramid of sound, paused, then modulated, *mezzo forte,* to the key of G. He played the opening phrase of the Doxology.

Below, the Reverend stretched out his hands, palms up, and the congregation took its feet with a rustling and crackling. An instant of silence filled the church. Then the singing began.

Mr. Moffat led them through the hymn, his right hand pacing off the simple route. In the third phrase an adjoining key moved down with the one he pressed and an alien dissonance blurred the chord. The old man's fingers twitched; the dissonance faded.

"Praise Father, Son and Holy Ghost."

The people capped their singing with a lingering amen. Mr. Moffat's fingers lifted from the manuals, he switched the motor off, the nave remurmured with the crackling rustle and the dark-robed Reverend raised his hands to grip the pulpit railing.

"Dear Heavenly Father," he said, "we, Thy children, meet with Thee today in reverent communion."

Up in the loft, a bass note shuddered faintly.

Mr. Moffat hitched up, gasping. His gaze jumped to the switch (off), to the air-gauge needle (motionless), toward the motor room (still).

"*You heard that?*" he whispered.

"Seems like I did," said Wendall.

"*Seems?*" said Mr. Moffat tensely.

"Well . . ." Wendall reached over to flick a nail against the air dial. Nothing happened. Grunting, he turned and started toward the motor room. Mr. Moffat rose and tiptoed after him.

"Looks dead to me," said Wendall.

"*I hope so,*" Mr. Moffat answered. He felt his hands begin to shake.

The offertory should not be obtrusive but form a staidly moving background for the clink of coins and whispering of bills. Mr. Moffat knew this well. No man put holy tribute to music more properly than he.

Yet, that morning . . .

The discords surely were not his. Mistakes were rare for Mr. Moffat. The keys resisting, throbbing beneath his touch like things alive; was that imagined? Cords thinned to fleshless octaves, then, moments later, thick with sound; was it he? The old man sat, rigid, hearing the music stir unevenly in the air. Ever since the Responsive Reading had ended and he'd turned the organ on again, it seemed to possess almost a willful action.

Mr. Moffat turned to whisper to his cousin.

Suddenly, the needle of the other gauge jumped from *mezzo* to *forte* and the volume flared. The old man felt his stomach muscles clamp. His pale hands jerked from the keys and, for a second, there was only the muffled sound of ushers' feet and money falling into baskets.

Then Mr. Moffat's hands returned and the offertory murmured once again, refined and inconspicuous. The old man noticed, below, faces turning, tilting upward curiously and a jaded pressing rolled in his lips.

"Listen," Wendall said when the collection was over, "how do you *know* it isn't you?"

"Because it isn't," the old man whispered back. "It's *her*."

"That's crazy," Wendall answered. "Without you playing, she's just a contraption."

"No," said Mr. Moffat, shaking his head. "*No*. She's more."

"Listen," Wendall said, "you said you were bothered because they're getting rid of her."

The old man grunted.

"So," said Wendall, "I think you're doing these things yourself, unconscious-like."

The old man thought about it. Certainly, she was an instrument; he knew that. Her soundings were governed by his feet and fingers, weren't they? Without them, she was, as

Wendall had said, a contraption. Pipes and levers and static rows of keys; knobs without function, arm-long pedals and pressuring air.

"Well, what do you think?" asked Wendall.

Mr. Moffat looked down at the nave.

"Time for the Benediction," he said.

In the middle of the Benediction postlude, the *swell to great stop* pushed out and, before Mr. Moffat's jabbing hand had shoved it in again, the air resounded with a thundering of horns, the church air was gorged with swollen, trembling sound.

"*It wasn't me*," he whispered when the postlude was over, "*I saw it move by itself.*"

"Didn't see it," Wendall said.

Mr. Moffat looked below where the Reverend had begun to read the words of the next hymn.

"*We've got to stop the service*," he whispered in a shaking voice.

"We can't do that," said Wendall.

"But something's going to happen, I know it," the old man said.

"What can happen?" Wendall scoffed. "A few bad notes is all."

The old man sat tensely, staring at the keys. In his lap his hands wrung silently together. Then, as the Reverend finished reading, Mr. Moffat played the opening phrase of the hymn. The congregation rose and, following that instant's silence, began to sing.

This time no one noticed but Mr. Moffat.

Organ tone possesses what is called "inertia," an impersonal character. The organist cannot change this tonal quality; it is inviolate.

Yet, Mr. Moffat clearly heard, reflected in the music, his own disquiet. Hearing it sent chills of prescience down his spine. For thirty years he had been organist here. He knew the workings of the organ better than any man. Its pressures and reactions were in the memory of his touch.

That morning, it was a strange machine he played on.

A machine whose motor, when the hymn was ended, would not stop.

"Switch it off again," Wendall told him.

"I *did*," the old man whispered frightenedly.

"*Try it again.*"

Mr. Moffat pushed the switch. The motor kept running. He pushed the switch again. The motor kept running. He clenched his teeth and pushed the switch a seventh time.

The motor stopped.

"*I don't like it*," said Mr. Moffat faintly.

"Listen, I've seen this before," said Wendall. "When you push the switch across the slot, it pushes a copper contact across some porcelain. That's what joins the wires so the current can flow.

"Well, you push that switch enough times, it'll leave a copper residue on the porcelain so's the current can move across it. Even when the switch is off. I've seen it before."

The old man shook his head.

"She *knows*," he said.

That's *crazy*," Wendall said.

"*Is it?*"

They were in the motor room. Below, the Reverend was delivering his sermon.

"Sure it is," said Wendall. "She's an organ, not a person."

"I don't know anymore," said Mr. Moffat hollowly.

"Listen," Wendall said, "you want to know what it probably is?"

"She knows they want her out of here," the old man said. "That's what it is."

"Oh, come on," said Wendall, twisting impatiently, "I'll tell you what it is. This is an old church—and this old organ's been shaking the walls for eighty years. Eighty years of that and walls are going to start warping, floors are going to start settling. And when the floor settles, this motor here starts tilting and wires go and there's arcing."

"Arcing?"

"Yes," said Wendall. "Electricity jumping across gaps."

"I don't see," said Mr. Moffat.

"All this here extra electricity gets into the motor," Wendall said. "There's electromagnets in these relay machines. Put more electricity into them, there'll be more force. Enough to cause those things to happen maybe."

"Even if it's so," said Mr. Moffat, "why is she fighting me?"

"Oh, stop talking like that," said Wendall.

"But I know," the old man said, "I *feel*."

"It needs repairing is all," said Wendall. "Come on, let's go outside. It's hot in here."

Back on his bench, Mr. Moffat sat motionless, staring at the keyboard steps.

Was it true, he wondered, that everything was as Wendall had said—partly due to faulty mechanics, partly due to him? He mustn't jump to rash conclusions if this were so. Certainly, Wendall's explanations made sense.

Mr. Moffat felt a tingling in his head. He twisted slightly, grimacing.

Yet, there were these things which happened: the keys going down by themselves, the stop pushing out, the volume flaring, the sound of emotion in what should be emotionless. Was this mechanical defect; or was this defect on his part? It seemed impossible.

The prickling stir did not abate. It mounted like a flame. A restless murmur fluttered in the old man's throat. Beside him, on the bench, his fingers twitched.

Still, things might not be so simple, he thought. Who could say conclusively that the organ was nothing but inanimate machinery? Even if what Wendall had said were true, wasn't it feasible that these very factors might have given strange comprehension to the organ? Tilting floors and ruptured wires and arcing and overcharged electromagnets— mightn't these have bestowed cognizance?

Mr. Moffat sighed and straightened up. Instantly, his breath was stopped.

The nave was blurred before his eyes. It quivered like a gelatinous haze. The congregation had been melted, run together. They were welded substance in his sight. A cough he heard was a hollow detonation miles away. He tried to move but couldn't. Paralyzed, he sat there.

And it came.

It was not thought in words so much as raw sensation. It

pulsed and tremored in his mind electrically. *Fear—Dread—Hatred*—all cruelly unmistakable.

Mr. Moffat shuddered on the bench. Of himself, there remained only enough to think, in horror—*She does know!* The rest was lost beneath overcoming power. It rose up higher, filling him with black contemplations. The church was gone, the congregation gone, the Reverend and Wendall gone. The old man pendulumed above a bottomless pit while fear and hatred, like dark winds, tore at him possessively.

"Hey, what's wrong?"

Wendall's urgent whisper jarred him back. Mr. Moffat blinked.

"What happened?" he asked.

"You were turning on the organ."

"Turning on—?"

"And *smiling*," Wendall said.

There was a trembling sound in Mr. Moffat's throat. Suddenly, he was aware of the Reverend's voice reading the words of the final hymn.

"*No,*" he murmured.

"What is it?" Wendall asked.

"*I can't turn her on.*"

"What do you mean?"

"I *can't.*"

"Why?"

"I don't know. I just—"

The old man felt his breath thinned as, below, the Reverend ceased to speak and looked up, waiting. No, thought Mr. Moffat. No, I *mustn't.* Premonition clamped a frozen hand on him. He felt a scream rising in his throat as he watched his hand reach forward and push the switch.

The motor started.

Mr. Moffat began to play. Rather, the organ seemed to play, pushing up or drawing down his fingers at its will. Amorphous panic churned the old man's insides. He felt an overpowering urge to switch the organ off and flee.

He played on.

He started as the singing began. Below, armied in their pews, the people sang, elbow to elbow, the wine-red hymnals in their hands.

"*No*," gasped Mr. Moffat.

Wendall didn't hear him. The old man sat staring as the pressure rose. He watched the needle of the volume gauge move past *mezzo* toward *forte*. A dry whimper filled his throat. No, please, he thought, *please.*

Abruptly, the *swell to great* stop slid out like the head of some emerging serpent. Mr. Moffat thumbed it in desperately. The *swell unison* button stirred. The old man held it in; he felt it throbbing at his finger pad. A dew of sweat broke out across his brow. He glanced below and saw the people squinting up at him. His eyes fled to the volume needle as it shook toward *grand crescendo.*

"Wendall, try to—!"

There was no time to finish. The *swell to great* stop slithered out again; the air ballooned with sound. Mr. Moffat jabbed it back. He felt keys and pedals dropping in their beds. Suddenly, the *swell unison* button was out. A peal of unchecked clamor filled the church. No time to speak.

The organ was alive.

He gasped as Wendall reached over to jab a hand across the switch. Nothing happened. Wendall cursed and worked the switch back and forth. The motor kept on running.

Now pressure found its peak, each pipe shuddering with storm winds. Tones and overtones flooded out in a paroxysm of sound. The hymn fell mangled underneath the weight of hostile chords.

"Hurry!" Mr. Moffat cried.

"It won't go off!" Wendall shouted back.

Once more, the *swell to great* stop jumped forward. Coupled with the volume pedal, it clubbed the walls with dissonance. Mr. Moffat lunged for it. Freed, the *swell unison* button jerked out again. The raging sound grew thicker yet. It was a howling giant shouldering the church.

Grand crescendo. Slow vibrations filled the floors and walls.

Suddenly, Wendall was leaping to the rail and shouting, "Out! Get out!"

Bound in panic, Mr. Moffat pressed at the switch again and again; but the loft still shook beneath him. The organ still galed out music that was no longer music but attacking sound.

"Get out!" Wendall shouted at the congregation. "*Hurry!*"

The windows went first.

They exploded from their frames as though cannon shells had pierced them. A hail of shattered rainbow showered on the congregation. Women shrieked, their voices pricking at the music's vast ascension. People lurched from their pews. Sound flooded at the walls in tidelike waves, breaking and receding.

The chandeliers went off like crystal bombs.

"*Hurry!*" Wendall yelled.

Mr. Moffat couldn't move. He sat staring blankly at the manual keys as they fell like toppling dominoes. He listened to the screaming of the organ.

Wendall grabbed his arm and pulled him off the bench. Above them, two last windows were disintegrated into clouds of glass. Beneath their feet, they felt the massive shudder of the church.

"*No!*" The old man's voice was inaudible; but his intent was clear as he pulled his hand from Wendall's and stumbled backward toward the railing.

"*Are you crazy?*" Wendall leaped forward and grabbed the old man brutally. They spun around in battle. Below, the aisles were swollen. The congregation was a fear-mad boil of exodus.

"Let me go!" screamed Mr. Moffat, his face a bloodless mask. "I have to stay!"

"No, you don't!" Wendall shouted. He grabbed the old man bodily and dragged him from the loft. The storming dissonance rushed after them on the staircase, drowning out the old man's voice.

"You don't understand!" screamed Mr. Moffat. "*I have to stay!*"

Up in the trembling loft, the organ played alone, its stops all out, its volume pedals down, its motor spinning, its bellows shuddering, its pipe mouths bellowing and shrieking.

Suddenly, a wall cracked open. Arch frames twisted, grinding stone on stone. A jagged block of plaster crumbled off the dome, falling to the pews in a cloud of white dust. The floors vibrated.

Now the congregation flooded from the doors like water. Behind their screaming, shoving ranks, a window frame broke loose and somersaulted to the floor. Another crack ran crazily down a wall. The air swam thick with plaster dust.

Bricks began to fall.

Out on the sidewalk, Mr. Moffat stood motionless staring at the church with empty eyes.

He was the one. How could he have failed to know it? His fear, his dread, his hatred. His fear of being also scrapped, replaced; his dread of being shut out from the things he loved and needed; his hatred of a world that had no use for aged things.

It had been he who turned the overcharged organ into a maniac machine.

Now, the last of the congregation was out. Inside the first wall collapsed.

It fell in a clamorous rain of brick and wood and plaster. Beams tottered like trees, then fell quickly, smashing down the pews like sledges. The chandeliers tore loose, adding their explosive crash to the din.

Then, up in the loft, the bass notes began.

The notes were so low they had no audible pitch. They were vibrations in the air. Mechanically, the pedals fell, piling up a mountainous chord. It was the roar of some titanic animal, the thundering of a hundred, storm-tossed oceans, the earth sprung open to swallow every life. Floors buckled, walls caved in with crumbling roars. The dome hung for an instant, then rushed down and mangled half the nave. A monstrous cloud of plaster and mortar dust enveloped everything. Within its swimming opacity, the church, with a crackling, splintering, crashing, thundering explosion, went down.

Later, the old man stumbled dazedly across the sunlit ruins and heard the organ breathing like some unseen beast dying in an ancient forest.

CLOTHES MAKE THE MAN

I went out on the terrace to get away from the gabbing cocktailers.

I sat down in a dark corner, stretched out my legs and sighed in complete boredom.

The terrace door opened again and a man reeled out of the noisome gaiety. He staggered to the railing and looked out over the city.

"Oh, my God," he said, running a palsied hand through his thin hair. He shook his head wearily and gazed at the light on top of the Empire State Building.

Then he turned with a groan and stumbled toward me. He tripped on my shoes and almost fell on his face.

"Uh-oh," he muttered, flopping into another chair. "You must excuse me, sir."

"Nothing," I said.

"May I beg your indulgence, sir?" he inquired.

I started to speak but he set out begging it immediately.

"Listen," he said, waving a fat finger. "Listen, I'm telling you a story that's impossible."

He bent forward in the dark and stared at me as best he

could through martini-clouded eyes. Then he fell back on the chair, breathing steam whistles. He belched once.

"Listen now," he said. "Make no mistake. There are stranger things in heaven and earth and so on. You think I'm drunk. You're absolutely right. But why? You could never tell.

"My brother," he said, despairingly, "is no longer a man."

"End of story," I suggested.

"It all began a couple of months ago. He's publicity head for the Jenkins ad agency. Topnotch man.

"That is," he sobbed, "I mean to say . . . he was."

He mused quietly, "Topnotch man."

Out of his breast pocket he dragged a handkerchief and blew a trumpet call which made me writhe.

"They used to come to him," he recalled, "all of them. There he'd sit in his office with his hat on his head, his shiny shoes on the desk. Charlie! they'd scream, give us an idea. He'd turn his hat once around (called it his thinking cap) and say, Boys! Cut it this way. And out of his lips would pour the damnedest ideas you ever heard. What a man!"

At this point he goggled at the moon and blew his nose again.

"So?"

"What a man," he repeated. "Best in the business. Give him his hat—that was a gag, of course. We thought."

I sighed.

"He was a funny guy," said my narrator. "A funny guy."

"Ha," I said.

"He was a fashion plate. That's what he was. Suits had to be just right. Hats just right. Shoes, socks, everything custom made.

"Why, I remember once Charlie and his wife Miranda, the missus and me—we all drove out to the country. It was hot. I took off my suitcoat.

"But would he? No sir! Man isn't a man without his coat, says he.

"We went to this nice place with a stream and a grassy plot for sitting. It was awful hot. Miranda and my wife took off their shoes and waded in the water. I even joined them. But him! Ha!"

"Ha!"

"Not him," he said. "There I was, no shoes and socks, pants and shirt sleeves rolled up, wading like a kid. And up there, watching amused, was Charlie, still dressed to kill. We called him. Come on Charlie, off with the shoes!

"Oh, no. A man isn't a man without his shoes, he said. I couldn't even walk without them. This burned Miranda up. Half the time, she says, I don't know whether I'm married to a man or a wardrobe.

"That's the way he was," he sighed, "that's the way."

"End of story," I said.

"No," he said, his voice tingling; with horror I suppose.

"Now comes the terrible part," he said. "You know what I said about his clothes. Terrible fussy. Even his underwear had to be fitted."

"Mmm," I said.

"One day," he went on, his voice sinking to an awed murmur, "someone at the office took his hat for a gag.

"Charlie seemed to pretend he couldn't think. Hardly said a word. Just fumbled. Kept saying, hat, hat and staring out the window. I took him home.

"Miranda and I put him on the bed and while I was talking to her in the living room, we heard an awful thump. We ran into the bedroom.

"Charlie was crumpled up on the floor. We helped him up. His legs buckled under. What's wrong, we asked him. Shoes, shoes, he said. We sat him on the bed. He picked up his shoes. They fell out of his hands.

"Gloves, gloves, he said. We stared at him. Gloves! he shrieked. Miranda was scared. She got him a pair and dropped them on his lap. He drew them on slowly and painfully. Then he bent over and put his shoes on.

"He got up and walked around the room as if he were testing his feet.

"Hat, he said and went to the closet. He stuck a hat on his head. And then—would you believe it?—he said, What the hell's the idea of taking me home? I've got work to do and I've got to fire the bastard who stole my hat. Back to the office he goes.

"You believe that?" he asked.

"Why not?" I answered, wearily.

"Well," he said, "I guess you can figure the rest. Miranda tells me that day before I left: Is *that* why the bum is so quiet in bed? I have to stick a hat on him every night?

"I was embarrassed."

He paused and sighed.

"Things got bad after that," he went on. "Without a hat Charlie couldn't think. Without shoes he couldn't walk. Without gloves he couldn't move his fingers. Even in summer he wore gloves. Doctors gave up. A psychiatrist went on a vacation after Charlie visited him."

"Finish it up," I said. "I have to leave soon."

"There isn't much more," he said. "Things got worse and worse. Charlie had to hire a man to dress him. Miranda got sick of him and moved into the guest room. My brother was losing everything.

"Then came *that* morning . . ."

He shuddered.

"I went to see how he was. The door to his apartment was wide open. I went in fast. The place was like a tomb.

"I called for Charlie's valet. Not a sound. I went in the bedroom.

"There was Charlie lying on his bed still as a corpse, mumbling to himself. Without a word, I got a hat and stuck it on his head. Where's your man? I asked. Where's Miranda?

"He stared at me with trembling lips. Charlie, what is it? I asked.

"My suit, he said.

"What suit? I asked him. What are you talking about?

"My suit, he whimpered, *it went to work this morning.*

"I figured he was out of his mind.

"My gray pinstripe, he said hysterically. The one I wore yesterday. My valet screamed and I woke up. He was looking at the closet. I looked. My God!

"Right in front of the mirror, my underwear was assembling itself. One of my white shirts fluttered over the undershirt, the pants pulled up into a figure, a coat was thrown over the shirt, a tie was knotted. Socks and shoes went under the trousers. The coat arm reached up, took a hat off the closet shelf and stuck it in the air where the head would be if it had a head. Then the hat doffed itself once.

"Cut it *this* way, Charlie, a voice said and laughed like hell. The suit walked off. My valet ran off. Miranda's out.

"Charlie finished his story and I took his hat off so he could faint. I phoned for an ambulance."

The man shifted in his chair.

"That was last week," he said. "I've still got the shakes."

"That's it?" I asked.

"About it," he said. "They tell me Charlie is getting weaker. Still in the hospital. Sits there on his bed with his gray hat sagging over his ears mumbling to himself. Can't talk, even with his hat on."

He mopped some perspiration off his face.

"That's not the worst part," he said, sobbing. "They tell me that Miranda is . . ."

He gulped.

"Is going steady with the suit. Telling all her friends the damn thing has more sex appeal than Charlie ever had."

"No," I said.

"Yes," he said. "She's in there now. Came in a little while ago."

He sank back in silent meditation.

I got up and stretched. We exchanged a glance and he fainted dead away.

I paid no attention. I went in and got Miranda and we left.

THE JAZZ MACHINE

I HAD THE WEIGHT THAT NIGHT
I mean I had the blues and no one hides the blues away
You got to wash them out
Or you end up riding a slow drag to nowhere
You got to let them fly
I mean you got to

I play trumpet in this barrelhouse off Main Street
Never mind the name of it
It's like scumpteen other cellar drink dens
Where the downtown ofays bring their loot and jive talk
And listen to us try to blow out notes
As free and pure as we can never be

Like I told you, I was gully low that night
Brassing at the great White way
Lipping back a sass in jazz that Rone got off in words
And died for
Hitting at the jug and loaded
Spiking gin and rage with shaking miseries
I had no food in me and wanted none

I broke myself to pieces in a hungry night

This white I'm getting off on showed at ten
Collared him a table near the stand
And sat there nursing at a glass of wine
Just casing us
All the way into the late watch he was there
He never budged or spoke a word
But I could see that he was picking up
On what was going down
He got into my mouth, man
He bothered me

At four I crawled down off the stand
And that was when this ofay stood and put his grabber
    on my arm
"May I speak to you?" he asked
The way I felt I took no shine
To pink hands wrinkling up my gaberdine
"Broom off, stud," I let him know
"Please," he said, "I have to speak to you."

Call me blowtop, call me Uncle Tom
Man, you're not far wrong
Maybe my brain was nowhere
But I sat down with Mister Pink
and told him—lay his racket
"You've lost someone," he said.

  It hit me like a belly chord

"What do you know about it, white man?"
I felt that hating pick up tempo in my guts again
"I don't know anything about it," he replied
"I only know you've lost someone
"You've told it to me with your horn a hundred times."
I felt evil crawling in my belly
"Let's get this straight," I said
"Don't hype me, man; don't give me stuff"
"Listen to me then," he said

"Jazz isn't only music
"It's a language too
"A language born of protest
"Torn in bloody ragtime from the womb of anger
    and despair
"A secret tongue with which the legions of abused
"Cry out their misery and their troubled hates.
"This language has a million dialects and accents
"It may be a tone of bittersweetness whispered
    in a brass-lined throat
"Or rush of frenzy screaming out of reed mouths
"Or hammering at strings in vibrant piano hearts
"Or pulsing, savage, under taut-drawn hides

"In dark-peaked stridencies it can reveal the
    aching core of sorrow
"Or cry out the new millennium
"Its voices are without number
"Its forms beyond statistic
"It is, in very fact, *an endless tonal revolution*

"The pleading furies of the damned
"Against the cruelty of their damnation
"I know this language, friend," he said.

"What about my—?" I began and cut off quick
"Your—what, friend?" he inquired
"Someone near to you; I know that much
"Not a woman though; your trumpet wasn't grieving
    for a woman loss
"Someone in your family; your father maybe
"Or your brother."

I gave him words that tiger-prowled behind my teeth
"You're hanging over trouble, man
"Don't break the thread
"Give it to me straight."
So Mister Pink leaned in and laid it down
"I have a sound machine," he said
"Which can convert the forms of jazz
"Into the sympathies which made them
"If, into my machine, I play a sorrowing blues
"From out the speaker comes the human sentiment
"Which felt those blues
"And fashioned them into the secret tongue of jazz."

He dug the same old question stashed behind my eyes
"How do I know you've lost someone?" he asked
"I've heard so many blues and stomps and
    strutting jazzes
"Changed, in my machine, to sounds of anger,
    hopelessness and joy

"That I can understand the language now
"The story that you told was not a new one
"Did you think you were inviolate behind your
     tapestry of woven brass?"

"Don't hype me, man," I said
I let my fingers rigor mortis on his arm
He didn't ruffle up a hair
"If you don't believe me, come and see," he said
"Listen to my machine
"Play your trumpet into it
"You'll see that everything I've said is true."
I felt shivers like a walking bass inside my skin
"Well, will you come?" he asked.

Rain was pressing drum rolls on the roof
As Mister Pink turned tires onto Main Street
I sat dummied in his coupe
My sacked-up trumpet on my lap
Listening while he rolled off words
Like Stacy runnings on a tinkle box

"Consider your top artists in the genre
"Armstrong, Bechet, Waller, Hines
"Goodman, Mezzrow, Spanier, dozens more
     both male and female
"Jews and Negroes all and why?
"Why are the greatest jazz interpreters
"Those who live beneath the constant
     gravity of prejudice?

"I think because the scaldings of external bias
"Focus all their vehemence and suffering
"To a hot, explosive core
"And, from this nucleus of restriction
"Comes all manner of fissions, violent and slow
"Breaking loose in brief expression
"Of the tortures underneath
"Crying for deliverance in the unbreakable
    code of jazz."
He smiled. "*Unbreakable till now*," he said.
"Rip bop doesn't do it
"Jump and mop-mop only cloud the issue
"They're like jellied coatings over true response
"Only the authentic jazz can break the pinions of
    repression
"Liberate the heart-deep mournings
"Unbind the passions, give freedom to the
    longing essence
"You understand?" he asked.
"I understand," I said, knowing why I came.

Inside the room, he flipped the light on, shut the door
Walked across the room and slid away a cloth that
    covered his machine
"Come here," he said
I suspicioned him of hyping me but good
His jazz machine was just a jungleful of scraggy
    tubes and wheels
And scumpteen wires boogity-boogity
Like a black-snake brawl

I double-o'ed the heap
"That's really in there, man," I said
And couldn't help but smile a cutting smile
Right off he grabbed a platter, stuck it down
"Heebie-Jeebies; Armstrong
"First, I'll play the record by itself," he said

Any other time I'd bust my conk on Satchmo's scatting
But I had the crawling heavies in me
And I couldn't even loosen up a grin
I stood there feeling nowhere
While Daddy-O was tromping down the English
    tongue
Rip-bip-dee-doo-dee-doot-doo!
The Satch recited in his Model T baritone
Then white man threw a switch

In one hot second all the crazy scat was nixed
Instead, all pounding in my head
There came a sound like bottled blowtops scuffling
    up a jamboree
Like twenty tongue-tied hipsters in the next apartment
Having them a ball
Something frosted up my spine
I felt the shakes do get-off chorus in my gut
And even though I knew that Mister Pink was
    smiling at me
I couldn't look him back
My heart was set to knock a doorway through my chest
Before he cut his jazz machine

"You see?" he asked.
I couldn't talk. He had the up on me
"Electrically, I've caught the secret heart of jazz
"Oh, I could play you many records
"That would illustrate the many moods
"Which generate this complicated tongue
"But I would like for you to play in my machine
"Record a minute's worth of solo
"Then we'll play the record through the other speaker
"And we'll hear exactly what you're feeling
"Stripped of every sonic superficial. Right?"

I had to know
I couldn't leave that place no more than fly
So, while white man set his record maker up,
I unsacked my trumpet, limbering up my lip
All the time the heebies rising in my craw
Like ice cubes piling

Then I blew it out again
The weight
The dragging misery
The bringdown blues that hung inside me
Like twenty irons on a string
And the string stuck to my guts with twenty hooks
That kept on slicing me away
I played for Rone, my brother
Rone who could have died a hundred different
    times and ways
Rone who died, instead, down in the Murder Belt

Where he was born
Rone who thought he didn't have to take that
    same old stuff
Rone who forgot and rumbled back as if he was a man
Rone who died without a single word
Underneath the boots of Mississippi peckerwoods
Who hated him for thinking he was human
And kicked his brains out for it

That's what I played for
I blew it hard and right
And when I finished and it all came rushing
    back on me
Like screaming in a black-walled pit
I felt a coat of evil on my back
With every scream a button that held the
    dark coat closer
Till I couldn't get the air

That's when I crashed my horn on his machine
That's when I knocked it on the floor
And craunched it down and kicked it to a
    thousand pieces
"You fool!" That's what he called me
"You damned black fool!"
All the time until I left

I didn't know it then
I thought that I was kicking back for every kick
That took away my only brother

But now it's done and I can get off all the words
I should have given Mister Pink

Listen, white man; listen to me good
Buddy ghee, it wasn't you
I didn't have no hate for you
Even though it was your kind that put my brother
In his final place
I'll knock it to you why I broke your jazz machine

I broke it 'cause I had to
'Cause it did just what you said it did
And, if I let it stand,
It would have robbed us of the only thing we have
That's ours alone
The thing no boot can kick away
Or rope can choke

You cruel us and you kill us
But listen, white man,
These are only needles in our skin
But if I'd let you keep on working your machine
You'd know all our secrets
And you'd steal the last of us
And we'd blow away and never be again
Take everything you want, man
You will because you have
But don't come scuffling for our souls.

'TIS THE SEASON TO BE JELLY

Pa's nose fell off at breakfast. It fell right into Ma's coffee and displaced it. Prunella's wheeze blew out the gut lamp.

"Land o' goshen, Dad," Ma said, in the gloom, "if ya know'd it was ready t'plop, whyn't ya tap it off y'self?"

"Didn't know," said Pa.

"That's what ya said the last time, Paw," said Luke, choking on his bark bread. Uncle Rock snapped his fingers beside the lamp. Prunella's wheezing shot the flicker out.

"Shet off ya laughin', gal," scolded Ma. Prunella toppled off her rock in a flurry of stumps, spilling liverwort mush.

"Tarnation take it!" said Uncle Eyes.

"Well, combust the wick, combust the wick!" demanded Grampa, who was reading when the light went out. Prunella wheezed, thrashing on the dirt.

Uncle Rock got sparks again and lit the lamp.

"Where was I now?" said Grampa.

"Git back up here," Ma said. Prunella scrabbled back onto her rock, eye streaming tears of laughter. "Giddy chile," said Ma. She slung another scoop of mush on Prunella's board. "Go to," she said. She picked Pa's nose out of her corn coffee and pitched it at him.

"Ma, I'm fixin' t'ask 'er t'*day*," said Luke.

"Be ya, son?" said Ma. "Thet's nice."

"Ain't no pu'pose to it!" Grampa said. "The dang force o' life is spent!"

"Now, Pa," said Pa, "don't fuss the young 'uns' mind-to."

"Says right hyeh!" said Grampa, tapping at the journal with his wrist. "We done let in the wavelen'ths of anti-life, that's what we done!"

"*Manure*," said Uncle Eyes. "Ain't we livin'?"

"I'm talkin' 'bout the coming gene-rations, ya dang fool!" Grampa said. He turned to Luke. "Ain't no pu'pose to it, boy!" he said. "You cain't have no young 'uns nohow!"

"Thet's what they tole Pa 'n' me too," soothed Ma, "an' we got two lovely chillun. Don't ya pay no mind t'Grampa, son."

"We's comin' apart!" said Grampa. "Our cells is un-lockin'! Man says right hyeh! We's like jelly, breakin'-down jelly!"

"Not me," said Uncle Rock.

"When you fixin' t'ask 'er, son?" asked Ma.

"We done bollixed the pritecktive canopee!" said Grampa.

"Can o' what?" said Uncle Eyes.

"This mawnin'," said Luke.

"We done pregnayted the clouds!" said Grampa.

"She'll be mighty glad," said Ma. She rapped Prunella on the skull with a mallet. "Eat with ya mouth, chile," she said.

"We'll get us hitched up come May," said Luke.

"We done low-pressured the weather sistem!" Grampa said.

"We'll get ya corner ready," said Ma.

Uncle Rock, cheeks flaking, chewed mush.

"We done screwed up the dang master plan!" said Grampa.

"Aw, shet yer ravin' craw!" said Uncle Eyes.

"Shet yer own!" said Grampa.

"Let's have a little ear-blessin' harminy round hyeh," said Pa, scratching his nose. He spat once and downed a flying spider. Prunella won the race.

"Dang leg," said Luke, hobbling back to the table. He punched the thigh bone back into play. Prunella ate wheezingly.

"Leg aloosenin' agin, son?" asked Ma.

"She'll hold, I reckon," said Luke.

"Says right hyeh!" said Grampa, "we'uns clompin' round under a killin' umbrella. A umbrella o' death!"

"*Bull,*" said Uncle Eyes. He lifted his middle arm and winked at Ma with the blue one. "Go 'long," said Ma, gumming off a chuckle. The east wall fell in.

"Thar she goes," observed Pa.

Prunella tumbled off her rock and rolled out, wheezing, through the opening. "High-speerited gal," said Ma, brushing cheek flakes off the table.

"What about my corner now?" asked Luke.

"Says right hyeh!" said Grampa, " 'lectric charges is afummadiddled! 'Tomic structure's unseamin'!!"

"We'll prop 'er up again," said Ma. "Don't ya fret none, Luke."

"Have us a wing-ding," said Uncle Eyes. "Jute beer 'n' all."

"Ain't no pu'pose to it!" said Grampa. "We done smithereened the whole kiboodle!"

"Now, Pa," said Ma, "ain't no pu'pose in apreachin' doom nuther. Ain't they been apreachin' it since I was a tyke? Ain't no reason in the wuld why Luke hyeh shouldn't hitch hisself up with Annie Lou. Ain't he got him two strong arms and four strong legs? Ain't no sense in settin' out the dance o' life."

"We'uns ain't got naught t'fear but fear its own self," observed Pa.

Uncle Rock nodded and raked a sulphur match across his jaw to light his punk.

"Ya gotta have faith," said Ma. "Ain't no sense in Godless gloomin' like them signtist fellers."

"Stick 'em in the army, I say," said Uncle Eyes. "Poke a Z-bomb down their britches an' send 'em jiggin' at the enemy!"

"Spray 'em with fire acids," said Pa.

"Stick 'em in a jug o' germ juice," said Uncle Eyes. "Whiff a fog o' vacuum viriss up their snoots. Give 'em hell Columbia."

"That'll teach 'em," Pa observed.

"We wawked t'gether through the yallar rain.
Our luv was stronger than the blisterin' pain
The sky was boggy and yer skin was new
My hearts was beatin'—Annie, I luv you."

Luke raced across the mounds, phantomlike in the purple light of his gutbucket. His voice swirled in the soup as he sang the poem he'd made up in the well one day. He turned left at Fallout Ridge, followed Missile Gouge to Shockwave Slope, posted to Radiation Cut and galloped all the way to Mushroom Valley. He wished there were horses. He had to stop three times to reinsert his leg.

Annie Lou's folks were hunkering down to dinner when Luke arrived. Uncle Slow was still eating breakfast.

"Howdy, Mister Mooncalf," said Luke to Annie Lou's pa.

"Howdy, Hoss," said Mr. Mooncalf.

"Pass," said Uncle Slow.

"Draw up sod," said Mr. Mooncalf. "Plenty chow fer all."

"Jest et," said Luke. "Whar's Annie Lou?"

"Out the well fetchin' whater," Mr. Mooncalf said, ladling bitter vetch with his flat hand.

"The," said Uncle Slow.

"Reckon I'll help 'er lug the bucket then," said Luke.

"How's ya folks?" asked Mrs. Mooncalf, salting pulse-seeds.

"Jest fine," said Luke. "Top o' the heap."

"Mush," said Uncle Slow.

"Glad t'hear it, Hoss," said Mr. Mooncalf.

"Give 'em our crawlin' best," said Mrs. Mooncalf.

"Sure will," said Luke.

"Dammit," said Uncle Slow.

Luke surfaced through the air hole and cantered toward the well, kicking aside three littles and one big that squished irritably.

"How is yo folks?" asked the middle little.

"None o' yo dang business," said Luke.

Annie Lou was drawing up the water bucket and holding

on the side of the well. She had an armful of loose bosk blossoms.

Luke said, "Howdy."

"Howdy, Hoss," she wheezed, flashing her tooth in a smile of love.

"What happened t'yer other ear?" asked Luke.

"Aw, Hoss," she giggled. Her April hair fell down the well. "Aw, pshaw," said Annie Lou.

"Tell ya," said Luke. "Somep'n on my cerebeelum. Got that wud from Grampa," he said, proudly. "Means I got me a mindful."

"That right?" said Annie Lou, pitching bosk blossoms in his face to hide her rising color.

"Yep," said Luke, grinning shyly. He punched at his thigh bone. "Dang leg," he said.

"Givin' ya trouble agin, Hoss?" asked Annie Lou.

"Don't matter none," said Luke. He picked a swimming spider from the bucket and plucked at its legs. "Sh'luvs me," he said, blushing. "Sh'luvs me not. Ow!" The spider flipped away, teeth clicking angrily.

Luke gazed at Annie Lou, looking from eye to eye.

"Well," he said, "will ya?"

"Oh, Hoss!" She embraced him at the shoulders and waist. "I thought you'd never ask!"

"Ya *will*?"

"*Sho!*"

"Creeps!" cried Luke. "I'm the happiest Hoss wot ever lived!"

At which he kissed her hard on the lip and went off

racing across the flats, curly mane streaming behind, yelling and whooping.

"Ya-hoo! I'm so happy! I'm so happy, happy, happy!"

His leg fell off. He left it behind, dancing.